I0519619

TROUBLE

ON THE

STRAITS

MICHAEL MARNIER

Published by VisualStoryteller Press
Copyright © 2015 Michael Marnier

2nd Edition Copyright © 2017

All rights reserved.
No part of this book may be reproduced, scanned or
distributed in any printed or electronic form without
written permission.

This is a work of fiction. Names, characters, places and
incidents are a product of the author's imagination or are
used fictitiously. Any resemblance to actual persons, living
or dead, businesses, companies, religious entities, events
or locales is entirely coincidence.

ISBN-13: 978-0692447185
ISBN-10: 0692447180

CONTENTS

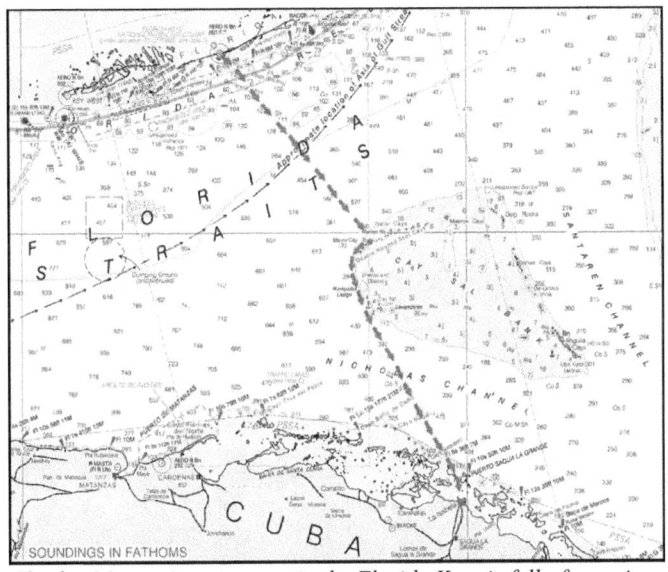

SOUNDINGS IN FATHOMS

Charley Manner's retirement in the Florida Keys is full of surprises. A shark sinks his boat. A dead man with a treasure map bobs up out of nowhere. And a Cuban drug lord shows up demanding the map. Charley's training as a former Navy SEAL prepared him for dangerous situations but this may be more than he can handle alone. Join Charley on a raucous ride from the Keys to Cuba and back, as he battles with trouble on the straits.

1

FISH TALE

THE REEL SMOKED HOT as the line screamed out nearly cutting off my fingers. I adjusted the drag and yanked hard to set the hook. The fish kept pulling like a tugboat hauling a barge in a riptide. On a good day, I've caught nine-hundred pound tuna and thousand pound marlin without breaking a sweat but this beast seemed intent on snapping my rod in half.

I planted my feet against the chair footrest and tightened my grip. "Gonna need a little help here guys."

Jake, my helmsman, started backing down the boat so I could gather in line. The monofilament stretched tight and sliced through the water, straight at the boat.

I hollered to Jake, "Quick. Shift to neutral. The props will cut the line."

Before she reached the stern the fish went straight down. My reel squealed like a pig when the drag brake failed and the line unspooled.

"She's diving for the bottom."

All I could do was lean back, hold on and hope the line didn't run out. It was a thousand feet to the bottom of the Wall. We were trolling for the big ones that come up to hunt near the surface.

I was harnessed into a new fishing chair. It creaked from the strain. My deck hand clambered down the ladder from the bridge and grabbed my shoulders. "She's too big, Mr. Manner. Maybe you should let her go?"

I consider myself a certified fish-fighting machine with the charbroiled tan and salt-crusted hair to prove it. "No way, Milo. I'll land this sucker. Throw more chum to bring her back up. And get the gaff ready."

I adjusted my grip and pulled, ignoring the burn in my biceps. The harness kept me from rocketing overboard.

Half way through a pull, the fish stopped. The line slackened. "Wait, she's coming up."

I dug my heels in, reset the drag and cranked hard but the line stayed loose.

"Damn it, she's coming up too fast." I cranked harder. "What the hell's this fish doing?"

Jake scanned the water from the fly bridge, pointed and said, "Look, Charley. Over there."

Ripples marked the surface behind us. She flashed a dorsal fin but that was all we could see in the murk. Might be a shark. The water over Cay Sal Bank was warm and cloudy this time of year. Dead plankton floated up the Wall from deeper water. Smelled bad but attracted baitfish. Bigger fish followed the schools of baitfish.

"How much line you got out, Mr. Manner?"

Still reeling in the slack, I checked the spool. "Only a hundred feet. Watch out, she's close."

"Do you see her?" Milo leaned over the port rail, straining to locate the fish. A violent crash sent him sprawling onto the deck. It felt like we'd run aground. No way, not in a thousand feet of water.

Eyes bulging, Milo got up, wiped his bloody nose and said, "She head-butt the stern."

This fish was serious. My twenty-thousand pound Ocean 35 Sport just got spanked by a fish.

It wasn't a blue marlin, that's for sure. Much bigger. I caught a glimpse of her razor teeth when the Great White lunged from the water and bit into the transom.

"To hell with this shit, get the rifle, and hurry." Milo scrambled to get my Colt carbine from the storage locker below deck.

The shark bit again, shaking violently side to side. My old boat couldn't take the punishment. The hull split along the keel. The ripping sound nearly drowned out Milo's shout. "Bilge pumps failed."

Water gushed from below to the aft-deck, washing empty tequila bottles past my feet. Oh shit. We're going down.

The boat shuddered and groaned as we listed to starboard. The shark stopped chewing on the transom but the damage was done.

I tried to release the chair harness. "Damn … the buckle's jammed." I looked around for some help but Milo and Jake were nowhere in sight.

I grabbed a fillet knife from the side pocket on the chair. Before I could cut the harness, both engines exploded, seconds apart, like a double-barrel shot gun. The force of the blast snapped the pedestal mount and catapulted me and the chair clear of the hull. The knife slipped from my grasp mid-flight.

Stunned after a belly-flop landing, still strapped in the chair, I rolled myself upright and called out, "Jake ... Milo, can you hear me?" No answer. All I heard was ringing in my ears. I hoped they got clear before the engines blew.

I watched my boat founder and break in two. The pieces tilted bow up, posed for one last photo op and slipped beneath the waves.

Spilled diesel had caught fire when hot fragments of engine metal rained back to the water. Smoke obscured my view as the waves washed over me, serving a foul soup of oil and chum bait. I gagged at the taste and spat it out.

I finally loosened the harness and reached behind me. Pushing on the footrest for leverage, I twisted around and switched on the EPIRB emergency beacon. It was mounted in a rod tube on the chair's back shelf. *No problemo*. Just needed to stay alive till the Coast Guard arrived.

I stuck my hand in the water to open the tackle drawer underneath the shelf and grabbed a bottle of tequila. It survived the blast and best of all, it was full. Unfortunately, no lime or ice. Plenty of salt, though. If you don't mind the chummy diesel aftertaste.

The seat cushions sandwiched between my butt and the chair kept me above the water line, but not by much. My legs dangled over the sides.

I took a few swallows of tequila. My palate cleansed of oil and chum, I focused on the bigger problem. Where the hell was the shark? I felt something slide against my leg and yanked it out, half-expecting to see a bloody stub. Negatory, just a hunk of seaweed wrapped around my ankle.

The wind shifted, pushing patches of fire in my direction. The smoke stung my eyes. I wiped them with my sleeve and looked up to see a fin rise between the swells. A very large dorsal fin with a tail fin trailing twenty feet behind. Definitely a big shark. I've been trained to stay cool under stress but I didn't see a way out. The Taliban couldn't break me but this shark certainly will, into bite sized pieces. I pulled my other leg out of the water, wrapped my arms around my knees and hoped the beast was just curious.

She cruised up to the chair at half throttle and bumped the bottom. The stainless steel spindle vibrated when sandpaper skin scraped past. Evidently, she had a thing for metal and clamped on to it after she turned and made a second pass. I filled my lungs one last time before she dove deep.

Here we go, Nantucket sleigh ride, except this one required holding my breath. My choice was abandon chair or hang on and hope for the best.

Well, sometimes hope does deliver the best. I looked over the edge of the chair and spotted a gap between her teeth. Big enough to fit the bottle I still clutched in my hand. I reached down and shoved the half-gallon of Gran Patron Platinum between her jaws. She bit harder and shattered the bottle, swallowing its contents. That's nearly three dozen shots of 90-proof tequila, accounting for the few pulls I partook earlier. Even a 4000-pound fish can't handle that much alcohol in one gulp.

She released the chair, and I bobbed to the surface. The shark just floated nearby, stunned by the jolt of alcohol. I craned my neck looking for Jake and Milo. Still no one in sight. They're both strong swimmers. If a rescue party comes soon, they may have a chance.

I heard the drumming of rotary blades before I spotted the Coast Guard rescue helicopter. It was locked on a beeline straight at me. Thank the fishing gods for EPIRB beacons.

The CG boys circled once before dropping a rescue litter. I kissed my chair goodbye and scrambled into the basket. A hundred feet up, swaying in the breeze, I scanned the area for Jake and Milo. Still no sign of them. I looked down and saw the shark thrashing around the chair. Her tequila buzz must have worn off. Maybe there'll be enough left to salvage but the boat's gone for good I'm afraid. I hope Yacht Insurance of Paraguay pays up.

Once I got aboard, I discovered the chopper co-pilot was my buddy Hawk Handy. He would have been on my boat if he hadn't pulled Search & Rescue duty this morning. Lucky for both of us. It's not the first time Hawk's saved my bacon. I owe him my life after what happened in Afghanistan during our final tour. I still have nightmares.

We continued to circle the area in a spiral search pattern. After five minutes we swooped toward some wreckage Hawk spotted a half mile east. As we got closer, I saw arms waving frantically. Milo and Jake were clinging to a single life preserver.

After we lifted the boys aboard I begged the chopper pilot, "Take us back around. Can't we winch up my chair? It cost me eighteen grand."

The pilot looked at Hawk, who just shook his head and shrugged.

The pilot turned to me. "Sorry Charley, no room, no can do."

2

DEATH CHAIR

HAROLD 'HAWK' HANDY is the best. Anything for a SEAL teammate. He didn't hesitate a second when I asked him to bring me back out in his Fountain open bow, *Triple H*. I was soaked to the bone from my swim with *Jawselle*, but no big deal. BUD/S training with the SEALs was a lot worse. It was still early but I wanted to get the chair before salvage pirates scooped it up. Plus, a fog bank was rolling in from the west. If it gets too thick we'll have to turn back.

My chair floated a hundred yards off the port bow. A few patches of fog limited visibility, but the main bank stayed west of us. The EPIRB beacon made finding it a snap. The shark was nowhere in sight but somehow, the chair picked up a new passenger, and he wasn't moving.

"Where did this guy come from?"

Hawk shrugged. "Didn't see him when we circled the wreckage this morning."

We pulled alongside. I leaned over the gunwale for a closer look. The face was contorted, teeth bared, eyes wide open. The scalp was riddled with slices, exposing skull bone. More cuts covered the chest, arms and legs.

"Someone wanted this dude to suffer some serious pain." I looked back at Hawk. "How the hell did he get out here?"

Hawk grunted and looked to the south. "Maybe a drug cartel boat dumped him."

I pointed at the bone white wounds. "He must have bled out fast with all those cuts. I'm surprised the sharks didn't get him before he climbed into the chair."

"What do you want to do, CJ?" Hawk always called me CJ, a moniker that stuck from our SEAL days. Everyone else called me Charley ... good-time Charley.

The cursor on the boat's GPS screen blinked over a spot north of Deadman Cays. The chair had drifted several miles northeast since my encounter with *Jawselle.*

"We're in international waters, close to Cuban and Bahamian jurisdictions. I don't want to mess with authorities from either country. Bad enough my boat's a thousand feet down. I just want my chair."

Hawk just looked at me so I egged him on. "You're in the Coast Guard, for Christ's sake. That gives you authority to retrieve the body, right? And I have the right to recover my own property."

"I better radio in, get an okay from Marathon CGHQ first."

Two minutes later, after Hawk explained the situation to his commander, we had permission to retrieve the chair and body. Just needed some photos with Hawk's cell phone while the body was still in the water.

After snapping some beauty shots we hauled the chair into the boat with the dinghy winch. Kept the body in the chair, touching as little as possible. It fit in the empty dinghy bed on the forward deck.

I secured the load while Hawk scanned the horizon. "We better move. I don't like being this close to Cuba with a dead man on the deck." He keyed the return waypoint for Marathon into the GPS. I climbed into the passenger seat.

The rising sun had burned off the rest of the fog. I shielded my eyes from the glare. Turning my head away, I caught a glint of light to the west. There are dozens of uninhabited cays in that direction. I've fished most of the Bank and know there's a lighthouse, abandoned in the 1940s, on the largest of the group called Elbow Cays. Until the late seventies it was used as a lookout for spotting drug smugglers and a waypoint for Cuban refugees fleeing across the straits. Built almost two hundred years ago by the English, the stone structure was in serious disrepair, barely safe to climb. There was another flash. It came from the top of the tower. "Someone's watching us."

Hawk followed my gaze, raised an eye-brow and shoved the throttles forward. "Let's get out of here."

~~~

WE DROPPED THE BODY off at the Key Vaca Coast Guard Station in Marathon. The local law met us when we arrived. Deputy Sheriff Vince

Walker was part of a Marine direct action group our sniper team had over-watched in Iraq.

"Hooyah, Vince. Found a stowaway on my fishing chair. Looks like he ran into a chain saw."

"Hey, CJ ... Hawk. I heard the story from Commander Ryan. That chair of yours attracts trouble. We'll need statement briefs from both of you."

Vince motioned to the CSI Tech to board us and do her thing before they removed the body from the chair.

More photos were taken, everything was inspected for prints, blood and possible DNA evidence. An hour later they released the chair after body-bagging the stiff for transport to the Miami-Dade coroner.

I invited everyone off-duty to join Hawk and me at the Blue Parrot for drinks and lunch, paradise-style. Too bad for the dead man, but I owed the crew that saved my butt this morning. Maybe my tours in Iraq and Afghanistan have tempered my feelings about death. I live each day like it's my last. Take whatever fate delivers. I was alive and so was my crew. The dude was dead. Shit happens.

~~~

HAWK TIED UP at the dock in front of the bar and we went inside. The regulars had already gathered around, including Jake and Milo, joined a few minutes later by the Coast Guard. With free drinks, even my sister's main squeeze, Hilly, showed up. Jonesy, the bartender, asked me for the details of my shark adventure. Never shy about spinning a yarn, I took a drink and began my tale.

"There I was, adrift near Cay Sal Bank, a thousand feet of ocean below me. My boat was gone. No sign of Jake or Milo. All I had to stay afloat was my fish-fighting chair and a bottle of tequila to keep me company."

Everyone cheered. Not for me or my missing crew. They were delighted I had a drink to sustain me. That's the way drinking buddies think. Before I continued, I rubbed my bruised stomach where the harness had dug in.

Hilly snorted, "Is this another fish tale? I'll bet you sunk your old boat for the insurance money."

I chose to ignore Hilly's dig. A groan filtered through the bar as I looked at my mates' raised eyebrows. I just smiled and shrugged.

Each man, except Hilly, licked salt from the back of his hand, tossed back a shot, and bit into a slice of lime. Hilly sipped his SoCo and sulked. He never believed my stories. I was used to it. Mostly I amused myself anyway. I looked around once more. "Shall I go on, boys?"

Hawk slammed his empty glass on the bar. "Back up, CJ. Tell 'em how you got in the water."

I knocked back another shot and continued, "My boat went down within a minute of the strike. I had hooked a twenty-foot Great White near the Wall. She took offense and ripped open the transom of my boat. I was strapped into my new fishing chair when the old boat broke apart and the engines blew. Lucky for me, the chair-spindle snapped away from the deck, catapulting me clear of the hull."

I smiled at Jonesy. "The teak tackle drawer and ladder-back options you recommended helped me stay afloat. I know, I know. I thought the price was too steep. Eighteen grand for the whole kit. Thanks. Money well-spent, especially the drawer that held a bottle of tequila. It turned out to be a lifesaver."

Hilly interrupted, "I'll bet the shark was really a piece of driftwood caught in the props."

I let out a sigh, "Come on, Hilly. Let me tell my story."

Hilly smirked and sipped his SoCo.

I continued, "A dorsal fin rose between the swells headed straight for me. The shark nudged the side of the chair and turned. I could hear her teeth click against the stainless steel spindle. I had to choose abandoning my chair-lifeboat or hang on and fight.

"So I shoved the half-gallon bottle of Gran Patron Platinum between her jaws. Nearly three dozen shots, not counting what I'd already drank. When the bottle shattered between *Jawselle's* teeth she just floated there with a smile that rivaled Julia Roberts' *Pretty Woman*."

I looked around at a dozen skeptical faces. Hawk rolled his eyes. I continued. "Lucky fisherman that I am, when she released the chair I bobbed to the surface just in time to flag down Hawk in the Coast Guard chopper."

A rousing cheer resounded off the walls—for my rescuers, certainly not for me—followed by the sound of empty glasses smacking the bar. That's how the late morning sloshed into mid-afternoon at the Blue Parrot, fueled by a case of Gran Patron.

Hilly wasn't finished taunting me and threw another barb. "Hey Charley, didn't you and Hawk find a body in your precious chair when you went back to get it?"

"You really know how to throw a wet towel on a good fish story, Hilly. The stiff came out of nowhere. Not my concern. He's on his way to the Miami-Dade morgue. Let them figure it out."

Hilly just scowled and took another sip of his SoCo.

For those of you that are color blind and possibly three sheets to the wind, the Blue Parrot Bar in Marathon should not be confused with the Green Parrot Bar—formerly known as the Brown Derby born back in 1897—the one on the corner of Southard and Whitehead in Key West. For one thing, old Blue has fewer *turistas*. Fine with me. A more intimate ambiance.

Marathon is actually a city spread out on seven keys, halfway from Miami, about fifty miles from Key West. A lot of keys, but still sparsely populated. After fifteen years of black-ops missions, I appreciated the peace and quiet. Plus, the bar is located right on the marina docks, with a panoramic view of the Florida Straits at no extra charge. My favorite hangout when I'm not offshore fishing in my boat ... I mean former boat.

After the rescue celebration wound down and the alcohol wore off with the assistance of some conch stew and grilled bonefish, Hawk and I returned to his boat and the fighting chair. I jumped into the seat behind the center console. "Let's get this over to my RV and check out the damage. I want to wash it down to get the salt and blood out of the fittings."

Hawk was about to cast off when he noticed the EPIRB on the chair was still powered up. He switched it off and looked around. "You know the glint you spotted? Anyone could have tracked us by following the EPIRB beacon."

Given my re-enactment of a *Jaws* movie scene took place only thirty miles from Cuba, and the sorry state of the corpse we found, I had an uneasy feeling. From the way Hawk was checking our six, I could tell he did too.

3

DEAD MAN'S MAP

HAWK STEERED TRIPLE H into my empty slip at the end of D-dock. My permanent RV spot was adjacent to the slip. A convenience that took me a year to arrange, with a little help from Jack Daniels. The marina owner is partial to Vets and appreciates good Tennessee whiskey. You might say I charmed my way into the arrangement with my gift for storytelling. Okay, I'll be honest. Jack did the heavy lifting.

After we off-loaded the chair I removed the EPIRB. As I pulled it out of the rod tube, I noticed a wadded-up swatch of oilcloth tucked behind it.

Hawk looked over my shoulder as I unfolded it on the dock. I grabbed a towel and blotted away the moisture. It was blank.

Hawk said, "Turn it over."

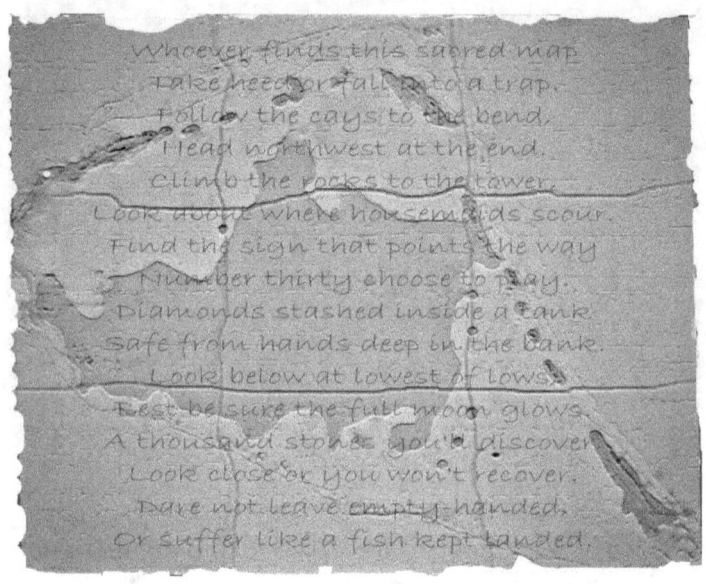

Whoever finds this sacred map
Take heed or fall into a trap.
Follow the cays to the bend.
Head northwest at the end.
Climb the rocks to the tower.
Look about where housemaids scour.
Find the sign that points the way
To number thirty choose to play.
Diamonds stashed inside a tank.
Safe from hands deep in the bank.
Look below at lowest of lows.
Rest be sure the full moon glows.
A thousand stones you'll discover
Look close or you won't recover.
Dare not leave empty-handed.
Or suffer like a fish kept landed.

"It looks like a map."

"Yeah, a map to what? Buried treasure?"

I waved it like a flag and laughed. "You wish. Probably worthless."

"Let's take it inside for a closer look."

I placed the oilcloth on the Winnebago's dinette table and turned on the overhead light. Frayed on the edges with creases at the folds, many of the detailed markings had faded but the writing was clear.

Hawk pointed, "The triangular shape looks like Cay Sal Bank."

I held it closer to the light and read the scrawling print. "There's a warning about a trap. And you may be right about the Bank. The next two lines say *follow the cays to the bend, head northwest at the end*." I looked up at Hawk. "What the hell is this about? I mean, some of it's obvious. But seriously… a hidden treasure?"

Hawk took the map, held it close to his face to read it for himself. "Maybe not worthless after all."

"If it's real, it explains the flayed body. Tortured to give it up. The guy had guts to take all those cuts and still get away with the map. I'll bet he hid it where the sun don't shine."

Hawk dropped the soiled cloth and wiped his hands. "Not much good to him now."

I slid it back under the light. "It says *climb the rocks to the tower, look about where housemaids scour*." I pulled out a nautical chart that included Cay Sal Bank and put it next to the map. "See the small hole in the upper left corner of the cloth? That's one of the Elbow Cays, the one with the old lighthouse."

Hawk said, "I've been in that tower. It's ready to fall apart. Had to climb a steep path through the rocks on the northwest wall of the cay to reach it. Let's go back and have a look."

"The rest of the writing doesn't say much. It mentions *diamonds stashed inside a tank* and *a thousand stones you'll discover*."

"What do you mean doesn't say much? Diamonds? When do we leave?"

I looked at Hawk and grinned. "Slow down, Captain Kidd. Don't forget the glint. And the EPIRB beacon. Better we do some recon before charging off."

"Good point, CJ. Let's sleep on it and go 'fishing' Thursday or Friday after my S&R shift. Make a copy of the map and lock it up, and put the original in a plastic bag. It smells pretty bad."

4

SOMEONE WATCHING

CARLOS BANDINERA slid a flash memory card into the laptop computer, opened the video file and pressed *play*. A grainy image appeared with two men leaning over the side of a boat looking at something floating in the water. The view zoomed in close, showing them attaching a winch line to a fishing chair with a body in it. Carlos pointed at the body and said, "That is Juan, Señor Campinera."

Jorge Campinera turned the PC and leaned close. "Who are these men? Los Zetas?"

"The name of the boat is *Triple H*. The NOAH documented vessels list shows it is registered to Harold Handy. We tracked them to a slip at Marathon Marina."

"Where did they find Juan?"

"Near Deadman Cays."

Jorge frowned. "Is he alive?"

"I doubt it, Boss. You cut him up pretty bad. I didn't expect him to jump overboard."

"What about the map?"

"No sign of it. Juan escaped before we could continue the interrogation."

"You should not have left him unguarded, Carlos. I hold you responsible if the diamonds are not recovered."

"He passed out. Lost a lot of blood."

Jorge smiled and licked his lips. He reached into a pocket and grasped the smooth ivory handle of his knife. Flaying live bodies always gave him pleasure. Holding the weapon made him feel powerful.

Carlos watched the expression on Jorge's face and stuttered, "B-Boss?"

Jorge broke his reverie and scowled at Carlos. "Enough. He was ready to break."

"Yes, Boss. Do you believe his story about the DEA deporting his family unless he cooperated?"

"No one could lie with that much pain."

"For a mule, he was a sly one. Why did he hide the diamonds?"

"Who knows? Maybe to be sure his family was safe before turning them over."

Jorge stood and said, "Delaying payment raised my suspicions. And I was right but I thought it was Los Zetas interfering, not the DEA."

Campinera paced the length of the room, turned and glared at Carlos. "And so where is the map? If the men have it, you must get it back, or you will suffer more than Juan."

Carlos swallowed hard. "Don't worry. I'll get the map. And if they have found the diamonds, I will get them back."

Campinera's eyes narrowed. "You do that, Carlos. Now leave me."

Carlos backed out of the stateroom and returned to his fast boat tied alongside the mega yacht. Fifty minutes later, he dropped anchor a mile off the Marathon Keys and reached for his cell phone.

5

STRANGER CALL

HAWK WAS HEADED for the door to my RV when his cell phone rang. "Hawk here." His expression turned stone cold, a look I'd often seen when we were on a mission, right before engaging the enemy. I waited for him to say something. He sat back down, switched to speakerphone and put his iPhone on the table between us.

"—and your partner have something that belongs to my boss."

Hawk asked, "Who are you? How did you get this number?"

"My name is Carlos. You are the owner of a Fountain boat named *Triple H*, yes?"

"What's it to you ... *Carlos*?"

"If you are Harold Handy, you have a document you need to give back. And please introduce your friend. I know you have me on speakerphone. Where are your manners, Señor?"

I pressed the mute button. "This guy sounds Cuban. Bet he's the man behind the glint. He seems to know a lot. We better play along."

I released the mute button. "My name is Charley Manner, Carlos. You have us at a disadvantage. What do you want?"

"*Muy bueno*. I like a man that is direct. You and your friend have something of great importance to my boss. The man you found was about to tell us where he hid it but chose to go swimming instead. Not a wise choice in shark-infested waters. We could not see him in the darkness and thought he drowned. An unfortunate situation. Please tell me you have the map, Señor."

Hawk asked, "Just who is your boss, Carlos?"

"That is not important, Señor Harold. You need to understand your situation is serious."

Hawk was not known for his patience or his tact. That stone cold look came back as he said, "Listen up, Carlos. Nobody threatens us. Get to the point. And don't call me Harold. I go by Hawk."

"No need for anger. This is strictly a business call. You have something that does not belong to you. We want you to give it back."

I spoke up, trying to cool down my fearless friend, "And if we did have this so-called map, how would we give it to you?"

"We know where you live, Charley Manner. Señor Hawk's boat is in a slip at Marathon Marina. I am betting you live nearby. I can send a courier."

"Whoa, no one said we have a map, Carlos."

"That is unfortunate. We have a video of you and your friend hoisting Juan and a fishing chair into Señor Hawk's boat. Did Juan tell you about a map?"

I decided to bluff. "I'd check your video, Carlos. All we found was my chair, the EPIRB and a seriously bled out body."

"*Si*, the EPIRB. How gracious of you to leave it on. The signal made the task of finding you quite easy. Too bad Juan did not survive his swim. We will be watching."

The line went dead. Hawk and I exchanged WTF looks. So much for slow and steady recon. Better watch our six. Hawk saved the number before closing his phone. Carlos will be calling again.

6

MIAMI DEA

A TALL BRUNETTE walked up to me and Hawk as we sat drinking margaritas under the coconut palm outside my Winnebago. Her gait and clothes, the shoulder holster under her open jacket, signaled Fed. Her partner stayed in the car at the curb.

She flashed her badge. "Afternoon, gentlemen. I'm Special Agent Vicky Borne with the DEA. Are you the men who found a dead body near Cay Sal Bank two days ago?"

I put down my drink next to the open EPIRB and the new batteries I bought yesterday. "Affirmative. Any news on the identity?" I looked at Hawk and he got the message to play dumb.

"His name is Juan Madera, a known Cuban drug cartel mule."

"Why did someone cut him up like that?"

Vicky hesitated, then said, "We'd turned him and set up a deal to divert a large payment of diamonds for drug shipments. Someone leaked the plan."

Hawk and I looked at the EPIRB sitting on the bench but kept our mouths shut.

"Do you guys know anything about that?"

Hawk raised an eyebrow, then went stone cold.

I asked Vicky, "Why are you here?"

She remained silent and stared at me for a full minute. Vicky had beautiful eyes, yet I felt a bit unnerved. Finally she said, "I think you know, Charley Manner."

Uh oh. We've been burned. I turned on my best boyish charm. "Gee, Ms. Borne, we went out to get my fishing chair, a very expensive chair. The stiff happened to hitchhike a ride. That's it."

I don't think she was impressed. Vicky smiled. She had a beautiful smile.

She asked Hawk, "Why so quiet, Mr. Handy?"

"Call me Hawk."

"Okay, Hawk. You have something to say?"

"Negatory, ma'am."

"Well gentlemen. As ex-Navy SEALs, you both should know the surveillance capabilities of our government. It happens that one of the National Reconnaissance Office satellites scanned the Florida Straits and the Keys two days ago right about the time you two hauled a fishing chair off Hawk's boat. You were particularly interested in something you found in one of the chair's fishing rod tubes."

Hawk's stone cold look froze solid. My jaw dropped and a shit-eating grin emerged. I said to Hawk, "The lady gets to the point, doesn't she?" Hawk grunted.

Vicky's voice hardened. "You can show me what you found, Charley. And while you're getting it, Hawk can show me the call log on his cell phone. We know Carlos Bandinera called you. NSA recorded it. The caller mentioned a map."

Hawk's stone cold look melted like butter on a plate of spicy-fried conch fritters. Time to 'fess up, I guess. DEA, NRO, NSA—alphabet soup serving too much evidence to swallow without choking. I raised my hands, "You win Agent Borne. What do you want?"

"No more lies. I need the diamonds. We planned to GemPrint them so they would be traceable and then allow Madera to deliver. The DEA is well-equipped when it comes to following the money. Everything was in place until he disappeared a week ago."

"But Madera's dead. How will you complete the delivery?"

She looked at Hawk, then back to me. "I can't deliver what I don't have. Get the map."

Coming back out of the Winnebago, bagged map in hand, I asked Vicky, "Who is Carlos Bandinera? His accent sounded Cuban. Very polite, but deadly serious."

"He's a top lieutenant in the Cuban drug cartel led by Jorge Campinera. Campinera's the guy we want for organizing transshipments of Columbian cocaine through Cuba into the States. Juan Madera was our best bet to get hard evidence of a transaction."

Hawk said, "Looks like Madera's death by a thousand cuts put the kibosh on that plan."

Vicky frowned at Hawk and reached for the map.

I handed it over and asked, "Is that why you want to see this?"

"You're a quick study. Why else?"

I was hoping she came to hear my *Jawselle* fish tale first hand or maybe to ask me for a date. No such luck. Used it all, out on the straits.

Looking at the writing through the clear plastic bag, her brow furrowed. "Have you figured out what this means?"

"Not yet."

Vicky slipped the bag into her pocket. "I'll take this back to the lab in Miami. Maybe our analysts can figure it out. Thanks for your cooperation, boys." She gave each of us a close look, lingering a bit on me, or maybe I'm just wishing. As she walked to her car, Vicky glanced back and said, "We'll be in touch."

When the car pulled away from the curb, I said to Hawk, "Good thing we copied the map. When do you want to visit the lighthouse tower?"

Hawk looked around and spoke softly, "Better wait a few days. The Cubans, and now the Feds are watching us."

"I agree. My sister and Hilly are having a party this weekend and we're invited. The recon can wait till Monday."

7

LITTLE BIG SISTER

KATIE IS MY LITTLE, BIG SISTER; a foot shorter, a hundred pounds lighter and four years older than me. Growing up, I always had her at my back. Our mother died in a car accident when I was ten and Dad was always out of the country. We didn't know at the time that he was a spy for the DIA, but that's another story. Katie stepped in when grade school bullies tried to push her little brother around. She still looked out for me. I tend to be impulsive and get myself into dangerous situations. Katie was there to bail me out. Hilly's a good match for her. Both are stubborn, but Hilly usually gives up when Katie digs in her heels. They plan to make an announcement at the party.

~~~

TWO HUNDRED FRIENDS and neighbors crammed into the American Legion hall. When Katie has a party, she doesn't go half way. Every permanent resident on the Marathon keys has been invited. The loud music and spinning disco ball set the seventies theme for the celebration. Dozens of Key-dwellers drinking, dancing, telling tall tales—not me, of course—enjoying the party. Everyone except Hilly. He stood in a corner, biting the nails of his right hand, an untouched glass of SoCo on the rocks in his left. I worked my way across the dance floor, showing a few disco dance moves to anyone that noticed, ending up in front of Hilly.

"What's the matter, Mr. Hildebrand? Nerves curb your thirst?"

"I prefer Hilly, if you don't mind, little brother." Hilly wiped his brow and looked across the hall where Katie was laughing with some girlfriends and pointing at the disco ball. He looked up at me with a dead serious look. "Katie will probably kill me, but I want to tell you something before we make our announcement."

"What is it, Bro? Tonight's all about fun. Why so serious?"

"You know I love your sister very much."

"Yeah, isn't that why you two are announcing your engagement tonight?"

Hilly looked away for a second. "Well, in fact, we're already married."

"Say again?"

"You heard me. You're already my brother-in-law, *Bro.*" Hilly smiled, put his finger to his lips and said, "Mum's the word. We couldn't wait any longer, went to a JP last month. Everyone will know later but I didn't want you to be totally surprised."

"And I thought I was the impulsive one in the family. Katie is usually more deliberate when it comes to big decisions."

Hilly grinned. "I guess my worldly charms won the day."

"I have to admit, you are good for her and she is definitely good for you. Where are you going for the honeymoon?"

"We plan to sail to the Bahamas and do a little scuba diving."

"How long will you be gone?"

"About two weeks. Leaving tomorrow."

"Be careful, Hilly, and stay in touch. Don't take the southern route—too many pirates and drug smugglers."

"You bet, brother."

Katie walked over and grabbed Hilly's arm. "It's time to make our announcement."

The DJ spooled up a rendition of *Here Comes the Bride* and cranked up the volume. A waiter wheeled in a huge wedding cake with tiny palm trees swaying above plastic bobble-head statues stuck on top. The groom wore surfer shorts and sported a high wave haircut right out of the fifties and the bride's hula skirt wiggled from the motion of the rolling cart. A sweet couple.

Hilly and Katie shouted, "Surprise!"

Not to me but I faked it, gave Hilly a slap on the back and Katie a big hug. The night got louder and the celebration went past midnight. I wished them *bon voyage* and once again warned Hilly to be careful. He's an experienced sailor, but that's not what worried me.

8

TREASURE HUNT

THE INSURANCE CHECK arrived. A hundred thousand smackers. Not even close to what I'd sunk into the Ocean 35, but at least they paid quickly. Kinda weird considering Paraguay is landlocked in the center of South America. No ships within several hundred miles except maybe some fishing boats on the Paraguay River. And there's money to issue yacht insurance?

I'm not complaining. Their premiums were reasonable but they hid behind the d-word: depreciation, when it came to pay out. Well, I 'depreciate' their check anyway. They whined a bit about the size of my claim. Wanted to be sure all of the gear, except the fighting chair, was permanently lost in the Deep Strait. I suggested they could go after it, but a thousand feet of ocean discouraged that option.

Replacement costs will depreciate my bank account big-time. I've already placed a deposit on a new boat and lined up a loan. This check is the down payment. Hope it doesn't bounce.

~~~

MY NEW BOAT—a Fountain 38 Sportfish with quad Merc Verado 350's—arrived yesterday. A sweet ride. I named her *Too Fast For U*. Fourteen-hundred horses and a top speed of 85mph. My fishing chair fits in the center of the aft deck. I haven't mounted outriggers yet. Serious marlin fishing in the Deep Strait will have to wait. For bone fishing in the flats, I added two electric trolling motors, one at each corner of the transom. The broad beam of the boat allowed enough room, even with the four Mercs installed. None of the gear is necessary today. Hawk and I will fish for diamonds.

We left Marathon at 0600, two hours before dead low tide. I punched in the GPS coordinates for Elbow Cays.

At 0645 Hawk pointed to a small opening in the cliff ahead as I eased *Too Fast For U* up to a flat outcropping. A rusted vertical bar fastened to the side of a ledge served as a tie point. Hawk used a sliding loop bowline knot so the boat would rise and fall with the tide. We deployed four large fenders over the gunwales to keep my new baby away from the sharp-edged rocks.

The top of the lighthouse tower loomed a hundred feet above us. A silent silhouette as the pre-dawn sky brightened from ochre to brilliant red. How's that sailor's saying go? *Red sky in the morning, sailors take warning...?*

As we climbed the rocks, I glanced back at the receding tide. Plenty of time to reach the tower before dead low, and *look about where housemaids scour*. Hawk and I discussed what this might mean before we left Marathon. There must be a clue somewhere on the tower floor.

We followed a well-worn path up the side of the cliff to the tower entrance and looked in. Evidence of other visitors lay about—boot scuffs, discarded wrappers and cans. A heavy layer of seabird droppings added to the ambiance.

Openings in the rotted roof and broken windows let in the elements, covering everything with a layer of grime.

Starting at opposite edges of the first floor, we began a slow walk along a spiral path, tracing our mini-lights back and forth, pushing the dirt aside with our boots.

Fifteen minutes into our search, I noticed a slight depression, an arc-shaped line close to the center of the room. We dropped to our knees and scraped away the debris, revealing a full circle carved into the stone. In the center a diamond shape, with numbers on left and right sides and the bottom point—seven, fifteen and thirty. *Number thirty choose to play*, I pushed thirty, hoping it would trigger some hidden door. Nothing.

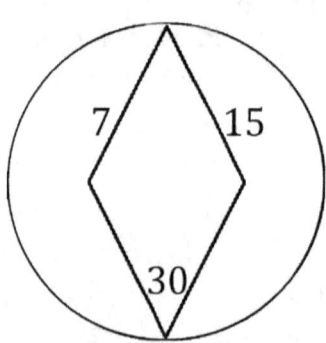

Hawk pulled out his SOG knife and started digging along the edge of the circular depression. "Looks like the edge of a door."

The blade sunk in about two inches as he dragged it along the arc. Halfway around the circle it stopped. Hawk blew away the dust. "A hinge ... and look there, another one. It's a trap door."

We both heard a metallic click and looked toward the tower entryway. "We've got company." I covered the crack and symbol with dirt and droppings then moved a few feet away. Hawk ran to the edge of the tower entrance, palmed his knife and hid behind the entry door. Three men rushed into the room, two with guns drawn. They didn't see Hawk.

The unarmed man spoke, "I told you we would be watching you. Where is your partner?"

I looked at the man. "Carlos Bandinera?"

"Si, and you are Señor Charley Manner, right? I do not recall telling you my last name when we spoke on the phone. Where did you learn it?"

"A fish told me."

One of the armed men started to walk back toward the door.

Carlos said, "Funny *gringo*. Have you found the map? Is this tower where our diamonds are hidden?"

"Come on, Carlos. We don't have any map. And what do you mean *diamonds*?"

Hawk sprang out and gave the closest gunman a high kick to the throat, snapping his head back, knocking him out cold. Still airborne, Hawk whirled and threw his knife at the second gunman before he could turn around. The knife sunk into his triceps but he still fired a shot at me before he dropped the gun. I felt the sting in my arm. No time to worry about it. I finished him off with my own high kick to the jaw. We needed to make a fast exit before more bad guys arrived.

Carlos stood still as I bolted past him. He just smiled and said, "We will be watching."

Hawk gave him a middle-finger salute, retrieved his knife and followed me back to the boat. Tied next to it, Carlos' boat sidled up to the fenders we'd hung over the gunwales. Hawk pointed at the foredeck. A mini-drone four feet wide sat there, micro-engines ticking as they cooled. It was similar to the backpack UAVs we used in Iraq. "So that's how Carlos knew we were here."

Blood dripped from my sleeve as I grabbed the tie line of Carlos' boat and wrapped it on an aft cleat of *Too Fast For U*. The bullet had grazed my forearm. I ignored it. Just a scratch. "Let's make it more difficult for them to follow." Once we cleared the rocks, I released the line.

An hour later, we pulled into Marathon Marina and headed for the Blue Parrot. Jonesy poured three shots of tequila, two for Hawk and me, the third to clean the wound on my arm. He dressed it up and served us conch fritters while we planned our next move.

9

A FAVOR

SHE SWAYED UP THE WALK and knocked on my RV door. This time she was alone. I had just taken a shower and put a towel around my waist as I opened the door. She stood under the awning to avoid the early morning downpour, her trench coat wrapped tight around curves I hadn't noticed the last time she was here. The coat barely reached her mid-thigh, accentuating a pair of long legs. I felt a rush as my blood pressure rose. "My favorite DEA agent. Back so soon?"

"Good morning, Charley. I bet I'm the *only* DEA agent you know. Can I come in?"

Guess she didn't care about my wardrobe. "Anything for the war on drugs. Step right in."

She closed the door behind her and twisted the deadbolt. "Look Charley, I know my visit last week probably ticked you off, but I need your help."

I smiled and tilted my head. "What do you really want, Vicky?" She looked at my towel and the slight bulge in it. I sucked in my gut. When was the last time I worked out? Never mind.

"I need hard evidence to nail Campinera and I need it fast. Our analysts have been unable to decipher the map. All they could tell me is a cache of diamonds lies somewhere on Cay Sal Bank, probably Elbow Cays but they're not sure. State Department flunkies contacted Bahamian authorities for permission to search but all I get is one delay after another."

She took a step closer. The smell of her perfume triggered a response from the bulge below my amidships. I dropped my hands in front, tried to look cool.

"What do you want me to do? Don't you have DEA assets that can help?"

"Only for stateside operations. I've got orders to stand down till we get Bahamian clearance."

She slipped off her trench coat. Her dress was a silk sarong, shorter than her coat, clinging to every curve, leaving little for my imagination. She pressed closer and placed her hand on my forearm. I winced as she touched the bullet wound. It had scabbed over but it was still tender. She looked at the ugly gash. "How'd you hurt yourself?"

"The bow line on my boat slipped from a dock cleat. I grabbed for it and got a rope burn."

Vicky raised her eyebrows. "I doubt that but I'm sure you can take care of yourself."

With one hand still covering a rising mizzenmast, I tried to stay on the subject. "So what do you want, Vicky?"

She cradled my arm, gently touched the wound with her finger tip. "Do you think you and Hawk could do a little *unofficial* recon at Elbow Cays? If I wait for the bureaucrats this lead will go cold and Campinera will slither away again." She pressed against the towel and looked up with those eyes.

I swallowed the drool forming in my mouth. "I'll speak to Hawk about it."

She elbowed me playfully in the ribs, loosening the towel a little, but it held fast around my waist. "You can call him as soon as we're finished."

I swallowed more drool. "I'm sure he'll want to help."

Clearly I was the victim of enhanced interrogation techniques. Putty in her hands but I kept my mouth shut about the encounter at the lighthouse. Hawk and I planned a second trip, this time at night, so it will be easy to accommodate her request. But not right now. I pulled her close. She wanted hard evidence.

10

SECOND TRIP

O-DARK-THIRTY, no moon and no wind; we approached Elbow Cays at idle speed. Back to the trap door marked with the diamond symbol and numbers. Under cover of darkness, our visit should not attract Carlos and company. Either way, we're armed and ready.

Hawk's SOG knife made quick work clearing the gap around the door. Using a crowbar, we lifted the slab without much trouble. A blast of cool air scented with brine whooshed out. The breeze pulsated in rhythm with the faint sounds of surf crashing on rocks.

I turned on my helmet-lamp and looked down the shaft. A metal ladder, wet with condensation and covered with layers of rust, was fastened to the wall. Climbing down, I concentrated on the slippery rungs, counting each one. Hawk stood at the edge above and fed out a life line. The shaft was just wide enough to fit my shoulders if I kept my arms extended above my head. The sound of surf echoed louder as I descended.

I looked closely at the seventh rung before putting any pressure on it. It was loose and wouldn't support my weight. I skipped over it. Same with rung fifteen. The verse on the map said to choose number thirty. Carefully, I applied pressure to the thirtieth rung. It held fast. I craned my neck around, looking for a likely hiding place, a loose brick or another sign. The curved wall opposite the ladder had another round door. It was set in a rubber seal. No handles. I leaned against it but it wouldn't budge. A few hard nudges on the left edge with my shoulder moved it a fraction of an inch. I pushed harder and it swung inward.

I leaned in and shone my light on the wall of what appeared to be a concrete cistern. Probably used for fresh water supply by the lighthouse keepers. At the bottom, dancing in the light, the water level rose and fell a few inches around several dislodged bricks, in sync with the waves crashing on the cay. I watched it for a few cycles. Each time, the level rose more than it fell. The bottom of the cistern must be rotted out to let in ocean water from below. The tide was coming in.

Hawk called from above, keeping his voice low, "CJ, you okay?"

"I'm okay. Found a door into a water tank. Going in for a look around. Hang tight to the line."

The inner wall of the cistern had no ladder. I slid over the edge using the life line to ease myself into the rising water. Opening the access portal must have sped up the inward flow. I scanned the walls, training my light in a spiral pattern as I tread water and rotated my body.

The portal was located about half way up the side of the tank. As I focused on the wall, looking for a hide hole where diamonds might be stashed, I didn't notice how quiet it got until it was too late.

The water level surged upward and slammed the door shut. It continued to rise, but slowed a bit. I guess the top half of the tank is a sealed chamber. I better get my butt out, before it fills. Even a pressurized bubble of air trapped at the top won't have enough oxygen to last very long.

I took a deep breath and dove down to the door. Grabbing the edges with my fingertips, I tried to pull it open. Too slippery. Too tight. The water pressure worked against me. The nylon life line hung loose as I floated back up to the shrinking air pocket. I dove again, grabbed the line and yanked three times. Hawk yanked back once to acknowledge. I yanked again three times, with greater urgency.

I floated back to the top of the tank for another breath. Only a foot left and the air was getting stale. I took what I thought was my last breath when the water level started dropping. I looked down and saw a size-15 tactical boot sticking through the open door. Water from the tank rushed out the portal and began filling up the access shaft. No time to look further. We needed to get out, now.

~~~

HAWK STARED DOWN at the water. It had risen to a point twenty feet below the floor. The access door into the cistern was ten feet below that. "I guess we need a new plan, bro."

"Roger that. I didn't see any openings inside except for the crumbled bottom. Before the tide came in, I could hear breakers crashing against rocks. There must be an opening that leads to the outer edge of the cay."

Hawk looked out the open window of the tower at the cliff we climbed. It was barely visible in the pre-dawn light. "If it's a tunnel big enough to make the water surge up so fast, it might allow us to make a water entry. Looks like fifty feet to the cliff from here. Too far to attempt holding our breath. Let's come back with diving gear."

"I agree. Now I understand what the map writing meant when it said look below at lowest of lows … the tide. With rebreathers, we won't have a problem."

Hawk and I kept our SEAL MK25 Draeger rebreathers when we retired. More stealthy than SCUBA. No bubbles plus it's worn on your chest. The low profile allows easier passage through small openings.

Back in *Too Fast For U*, before I cranked the engines, we both heard it. A high-pitched whine echoed off the cliff. Looking up, a mini-drone hovered behind a large boulder. We both waved as I started her up. "They must have night vision on that drone."

Hawk nodded and cast off the lines. Time to fly before Campinera unleashes Carlos and his goons. Vicky will be disappointed but I'll try to make it up to her. I wonder if she'll wear her trench coat again.

11

SNAGGED AND BAGGED

KATIE HUNG over the side, gazing at a school of tropical fish below their boat as she and Hilly set sail from Matthew Town, Great Inagua. Sixty feet of crystal clear water provided an unobstructed view of the coral covered bottom. The dives at the reef were spectacular, well worth the trip from Nassau. The final leg of their honeymoon cruise lay ahead. Hilly had checked the latest weather forecast and looked at his watch. "If we head northwest along the Old Bahama Channel we'll get home a day early. We can make a stop at Andros Island. What do you think?"

"I don't know, Horatio, that heading skirts the edge of Cuban waters. Didn't Charley warn you about pirates and drug smugglers on the southern route?"

"Yes he did, but I'm thinking that Cuban gunboat patrols will discourage illicit traffic. And I don't think the Castro brothers are interested in us."

Katie hesitated for a moment, then said, "Okay, you're the captain."

~~~

TWO DAYS OUT of Matthew Town, just past Cay Lobos, three gunboats surrounded the thirty foot sloop. Hilly maintained his northwest heading.

"I thought you said the Cubans wouldn't bother us."

"There's something not right about this, Kate. I've sailed this route before and spotted many gunboats, but they always left me alone."

"But we're not even in Cuban waters."

"Right, but that doesn't seem to matter this time. They're signaling to board. Hang on, I'm heading north."

One of the gunboats maneuvered directly in front, forcing Hilly to drop sails. Two armed men jumped aboard.

Hilly yelled, "We're in international waters, you can't board my boat."

One of the men responded by swinging his rifle butt at Hilly's head. Katie screamed as he went down on the deck. The second man tossed a bow line to the nearest gunboat. A southeast heading told Katie they were going to Cuba. She cradled Hilly's head after wrapping it with a spare tee shirt to slow the bleeding.

~~~

CARLOS BOARDED the mega yacht and entered the main cabin. Jorge Campinera spun his chair and motioned Carlos to sit on the couch across from him.

"Are the newlyweds comfortable?"

"The woman is fine … but very angry and won't shut up. Her husband has lost some blood and doesn't look so good."

"Make sure he receives medical attention. I don't want him dead, unless it becomes necessary."

"What's our next move, Boss?"

Campinera gazed at the gentle swells rolling in from the Atlantic, then turned to face Carlos. "You screwed up my interrogation of Juan, I do not trust your judgement anymore. I will fly to La Isabella tonight to visit our hostages personally. You will contact Charley Manner and arrange a swap. His sister and her husband for a thousand diamonds."

Carlos nodded and said, "The man has a deep gash in the head. When do you want to do it?"

"Have the wound sewn up and give Manner forty-eight hours. If he can't do it by then, kill the man and drop his body where it will be easily found."

12

RANSOM DEMAND

HAWK AND I MET for breakfast at the Blue Parrot. Last night's visit to the lighthouse wasn't a total bust. At least we understood more of the writing on the map.

Sitting in a booth in the back corner, away from other customers, we had just gotten our eggs and bacon when Hawk's cell phone rang. His stone cold look told me it wasn't good news. He showed me the caller i.d. and put it on speakerphone with the volume turned way down.

"Good morning, gentlemen. I do not have Señor Charley's number, but I suspect you are together. I have some bad news for him. But first, did you find our diamonds?"

I was hungry and didn't have patience for this guy. He better have a good reason for calling. "I don't know anything about diamonds, Carlos. What's the bad news?"

"It is unfortunate that you continue to play a game with me, Señor Charley. My drones can see in the dark. We know you visited the Elbow Cays lighthouse."

Hawk chimed in, "So what, Carlos. We were checking out the view."

"Not funny, and neither is the news I have."

"Come on, Carlos. Spit it out. Our breakfast is getting cold."

"Pay attention, Señor Charley. We have your sister and her husband."

I gagged on a mouthful of coffee. "Not likely, Carlos. They're still in Nassau last time I checked."

"You are mistaken, Señor Charley. They were floundering in their sailboat off the coast of Cuba. Foolish. Lucky for them we arrived before the sharks. Listen closely."

I could barely hear her voice. She was crying.

"Charley, these men are serious. Please listen to them. There isn't much time. Hilly's in a bad way."

"Katie . . . are you still there? What have they done to you?"

"Sorry, Señor Charley. You have forty-eight hours to find the diamonds."

The line went dead. Hawk and I exchanged battle stares. Time for aggressive action. I pulled out my phone and called Vicky.

~~~

VICKY DIDN'T WASTE TIME driving the hundred mile trip from Miami. She arrived less than two hours after my call. She came alone. I described what Hawk and I found beneath the lighthouse and the ransom call from Carlos. We're going back ASAP. Our return still must be unofficial. No word yet from the dweebs at State.

"I know you want to nail Campinera, Vicky, but the situation has become personal."

"I understand, Charley. You and Hawk need to do what you need to do to save your sister and her husband. I want to help."

"That's good to hear. Hawk and I have prepped our rebreather gear and borrowed

Jonesy's Chris Craft. No doubt the Cartel is watching the lighthouse. Going in daylight, we don't want Carlos and his boys to see us approach."

"If you do find the diamonds, what then?"

"You mean *when* we find them. I know we're close. With underwater gear, we'll have more time to search no matter what the tide level is inside the cistern."

"You said on the phone that you have only forty-eight hours. I happen to know Campinera just arrived at his penthouse in Miami. I have the phone number we monitor. We can use the diamonds to set up a face-to-face meeting."

"We'll see, Vick. I don't want to do something that will harm my sister. I doubt if she and Hilly are in the States, so we need to keep some diamonds as a bargaining chip."

Hawk said, "We better get moving."

The single screw Chris Craft is slower than our Fountain boats and we'll have a mile underwater swim to the cay.

13

DIAMONDS UP THE WAHOO

FIVE MILES OUT, we used high power watch binoculars and spotted Cartel goons standing around the tower base, automatic weapons slung on their shoulders. There were at least a dozen men. With a little luck our under water entry will avoid trouble.

One mile out, Vicky killed the engine and maintained a heading straight toward the cay. Hawk and I somersaulted off the stern dive platform. Our weight belts sank us to a thirty foot depth before we added air to our buoyancy compensator vests. Weightless and silent, we kicked toward the base of the cliff.

The Florida Current flows west to east so we chose our start point west of the target and used the current to glide in, conserving our energy and the capacity of our rebreathers. Vicky will power up and return to the drop point every twenty minutes, a classic drift fishing maneuver. She'll have a few lines over the side in case anyone looks in her direction. Last thing we want is a fight with heavily armed men. If they bushwhack us and take the diamonds, we won't get Katie and Hilly back alive.

~~~

WE REACHED THE EDGE of the cay below the lighthouse before noon. There was a fissure in the cliff wall, fifteen feet below the surface. The high tide kept our entry hidden from the men at the base of the tower. The tunnel was large enough for us to swim side-by-side until we reached the crumbled remains of the cistern bottom. The hole was not very big. Hawk stayed outside in case anyone else showed up. You never know. Always watch your six.

I pulled a few loose rocks to fit through the opening. Before sticking my head in, a fish burst out of the hole and sprinted for deep water. It was a wahoo, and a big one. How she got trapped in the small space is a mystery. I gave Hawk an OK sign and went in for a closer look. My dive-helmet light illuminated the tank walls. Picking up where I left off the last visit, I began a spiral scan around and around, working my way to the top. This time I spotted a three inch hole about two feet from the ceiling. It looked like a feed pipe. Maybe that's how the lighthouse keepers filled the tank with fresh water.

I shone my light straight down the sidewall below the hole and found another opening at the edge of the tank bottom. Missed it on the way in. Got to be the pipe used to pump water up to the lighthouse. I looked more closely at the upper pipe. Seaweed partially covered the opening. I cut away the growth with my SOG knife. About six inches in I found a rubber tube, the size of a pepperoni sausage, stuffed in with more seaweed. When I pulled it out there was a strong suction pulling into the cleared pipe. The water level started to drop. I remembered the end of the verse on the map.

> *A thousand stones you'll discover,*
> *Look close or you won't recover.*
> *Dare not leave empty-handed,*
> *Or suffer like a fish kept landed.*

By removing the tube the incoming tide water level in the tank would no longer reach the top. It would drain out the pipe, leaving a larger air pocket for anyone trapped to survive until the tide turned. They would need patience to wait calmly, conserving oxygen. Not a foolproof plan. I'm glad I didn't have to test it. Last time I had left empty handed, and would have suffocated *like a fish kept landed* if Hawk hadn't kicked in the portal door.

The tube had some heft to it but difficult to say how much underwater. I popped off the end cap and shone my light inside. Hooyah, sparkling diamonds reflected back. I resealed it. Time to leave.

I gave a thumbs up to Hawk when I emerged from the cistern and waved the tube. We swam back to the boat, kicking balls to the wall against the Florida Current. A large shadow moved below us, too deep to see clearly. No time for another drink with *Jawselle*. My sister and Hilly need to be rescued. We kicked harder.

~~~

VICKY WAS WAITING at the rendezvous point with the bow facing the cay when we surfaced. We climbed the dive platform ladder, slipped through the transom door and went below. I opened the tube and spilled the contents onto the forward berth in the cuddy cabin. Diamonds. Big diamonds. Hundreds by the look of it. There was something else.

Hawk pointed, "Is that another oil cloth?"

I unfolded it. No map this time. Just some writing.

> *One hundred more*
> *Swim off shore.*
> *Fish the right bait*
> *And do not wait.*
> *The carrier is alive*
> *But will not survive.*
> *Diamonds up the wahoo.*

I looked at Hawk. We both started counting the diamonds. We made separate piles of one hundred each. It took a few minutes.

"There's something fishy here, only nine piles. Juan Madera was a sly SOB. That wahoo's got the last one hundred diamonds. No time to catch her, we've got to visit Campinera, pronto."

I called up to Vicky at the helm, "Pull in the fishing lines and head back full speed, Vick. We're a hundred short but there's enough for drug lord bait." I scooped up the diamonds, stuffed them with the oil cloth in my duffel and followed Hawk up the stairs to the deck.

14

DRUG LORD'S LAIR

FIFTY FLOORS UP, Vicky and I stepped off the elevator. Two oversized bodyguards in undersized black tee shirts and camouflage cargo pants waved metal detector wands up and down our bodies. They didn't find the satin pouch concealed in Vicky's ample cleavage. She stared them off when they got close. We had brought only one hundred diamonds to start the negotiations. They were laser scanned by GemPrint. Every diamond has its own unique visual signature—like a fingerprint.

Hawk stayed in the lobby, holding another hundred in case we needed them. Vicky wore a wire—a tiny bug with wireless link to Hawk. He could hear and record everything. The stooges missed the bug, located in place of the third pearl button of her clingy silk blouse.

Jorge Campinera stood looking out a large window with a panoramic view of Biscayne Bay, ignoring our arrival. He couldn't be more than five feet two inches tall, and weigh one hundred forty pounds.

Make no mistake, his rep foretells a willingness to do violent things to get his way. Throw in a suspicious and egotistic nature and you have a very dangerous man. Vicky's file on him says he's seventy-two. Small and wiry, he fits the profile of a gangster with a Napoleon-complex. We better use some finesse—not my forte. I'll let my sexy partner take the lead.

He turned from the window, his stern Cuban features melted to a broad smile when he saw Vicky. He rushed up to her, took her hand and slobbered a kiss on her finger tips, keeping his eyes fixed on her breasts. He paid no attention to me. Not his type, lucky me. This could go well if I keep my mouth shut.

Jorge asked Vicky, "When Señor Charley said he would come with a friend, I expected his partner. I had no idea. Perhaps when we are finished with this unfortunate business, you might stay for some lunch?" He still didn't look at me, so I guess I wasn't invited.

I cleared my throat, "Allow me to introduce Victoria Barnes." Vicky suggested we use a fake last name. "She's a friend . . . a very close friend." Jorge still ignored me. I think he was sucking on Vick's finger tips. Gag me with chum bait.

"Victoria, such a beautiful name."

Vicky inhaled deeply, thrust out her breasts and smiled. I thought Jorge was going to have a seizure. I gave her a don't-overplay-it look. She just winked. Jorge thought it was for him. What a dork.

Jorge finally tore his eyes away from Vicky and spoke to me. "You said when you called that you found my diamonds. Where are they?"

"Where's my sister and her husband?"

Jorge's cheeks reddened.

Vicky stepped between us, elbowing me in the ribs, which reminded me of her visit to my RV and brought a smile to my face.

She batted her eyes at Jorge and said, "Please, Mr. Campinera, Charley's just upset. You know how it is when family is in trouble?"

The drug lord smiled at her, "Of course. He is upset. I hope *you* are not upset? And please call me Jorge."

Vicky pressed closer, "To be honest, Jorge, I am worried about Charley's sister *and* her husband. Charley told me Katie said something about Horatio needing help. Is he injured?"

Campinera waved his hand, "I leave such details to Carlos. If you have my diamonds, we can return Señor Charley's family without delay."

Vicky reached into her blouse and pulled out the pouch. Campinera's eyes bulged. She dangled it in front of him. Like a lizard thwacking a fly out of the air, he snatched the silk bag and held it to his nose, inhaling deeply. The lecher.

After a second lascivious lungful, a puzzled look came on his face. "This smells exquisite but there must be more. I lost one thousand diamonds. My business associate assured me there were one thousand five-carat brilliant cut stones, all grade D colorless, internally flawless, worth $100,000 each."

Vicky leaned forward for a better audio pick up. "You are certainly a man who knows rare gems, Jorge. I'm impressed."

Jorge puffed his small chest out and said, "I do enjoy the finer things in life and make it my business to know their value."

"Are you in the jewelry business, Jorge?"

"I am in any business that makes money. The diamonds were payment for some goods delivered to a customer. Unfortunately, the employee tasked to bring payment to me was dishonest."

I had to bite my tongue. Dishonesty has a variable meaning to this crook. Vicky, accomplished actress that she is proving to be, just flashed an admiring smile at this Napoleon wannabe.

Vicky said, "Charley told me about the corpse he found in his fishing chair. It must have been an awful accident."

Jorge Bonaparte beamed, "Oh my dear, with one-hundred million dollars in diamonds at stake, it was no accident."

Gotcha. Keep talking, coke-for-brains.

"I expect loyalty from employees. When they are disloyal, they feel my knife." Jorge reached into his pocket, but then stopped himself. He shook his head and looked at me. "Señor Charley, where are the rest?"

Vicky wasn't giving up control easily. She pushed herself against Jorge and said, "Oh Jorge, we brought these today as a gift, a sign of good faith. After all, you are not releasing Katie and Horatio right now, are you?"

He leaned into her advance and smiled. "You are correct. How rude of me not to recognize your generous gesture. When can you deliver the rest? Carlos will bring your friends to swap."

I couldn't keep silent any longer. The love fest was too much. "Tomorrow at noon. They better be healthy, Jorge." He seemed oblivious to my threat.

"No problem. I will instruct Carlos to be at the lighthouse tower with your sister and brother-in-law. It is better to do it on neutral ground, yes?"

Vicky gave him a squeeze on the bicep...a puny bicep. "We'll be there with the diamonds."

Jorge seemed pleased with himself and offered again for Vicky to stay for lunch and whatever. I still was not invited. Vicky wisely declined but asked for a rain check. We made a rapid exit, passing Hawk in the lobby as he gave us a thumbs up. He got it all on microchip.

15

THE SWAP

A FAST MOVING late season tropical storm roared into the straits overnight. Travel by boat was dangerous but circumstances demanded no delays. State Department flunkies finally gained approval from the Bahamian authorities to officially enter Elbow Cays. There was a catch. There's always a catch with the federal government.

Since the case had morphed into a kidnapping, Vicky had to welcome a new team member from the FBI. She called me late last night from her office in Miami. I had just gotten back to Marathon when my phone rang. She told me her goal remained gathering enough evidence to arrest Campinera for drug trafficking and murder, but she assured me that my sister's safe return was more important.

Hawk and I waited at the Marathon Marina, watching the breakers wash over the outer docks.

Hawk said, "Rough seas, bro. When is Vicky supposed to get here?"

"She should be here by now. We'll blow the swap if we don't leave soon. Sixty miles will seem like a hundred sixty with this storm."

Hawk pointed at the entrance to the main channel of the marina. "That must be her."

A forty-two foot Cigarette boat carved through the chop and idled into the empty slip next to *Too Fast For U.* Vicky waved from the passenger seat as a deckhand jumped onto the dock to tie up. A swarthy man dressed inappropriately for a rough sea passage emerged from the cabin. Hawk and I walked over for introductions.

Vicky looked stressed. "Good morning guys. This is Dino Bachero, FBI Special Agent assigned to the case." Her voice was laced with venom.

I tried to sound civil, "I didn't know we needed help. What's changed?"

Bachero blurted, "There's no room for mistakes. We want to rescue your sister and her husband unharmed *and* build the case against Campinera. Professionals can do it. Amateurs will screw it up."

Hawk went ballistic, "Who are you calling amateur, dude?"

I could see that Vicky was holding her tongue. Apparently she had no choice but accept Bachero to our team. In fact, it appeared he joined as *co-leader*. Talk about too many chiefs. If my Italian is accurate, *bachero* means dishwasher. I see a cluster fuck coming. But we had no time to debate who's in charge. We needed to agree on a plan and get underway. The rough seas will make it at least a two hour trip to Cay Sal Bank.

Bachero invited us to go below in the Cigarette's forward cabin. It was the 42X model, a go-fast boat with twin 700 horsepower V-drives that could push the sliver-shaped hull to a top speed of 100mph on smooth water. The purple paint job fit the name — *Purple People Eater*.

We decided to use two boats, one for backup will stay a mile offshore from the cays. The high winds and rain eliminated the chance of a mini-drone spotting the size of our group. The shallows of Cay Sal Bank will be exploding with breakers that will test our sea legs as well as our stomachs.

Dino was green around the gills after the trip down from Miami but still tried to gain control of the planning. He mistakenly thought his home turf advantage aboard *Purple People Eater* gave him the right. Vicky wouldn't have it. Before he could get a word out she said, "Campinera's been my number one priority for the past eighteen months. This is the break I've been waiting for and I'll be damned if you think you can take the lead, Dino."

The dishwasher's face reddened. "Ms. Borne, the Director made it clear we would act as a unified team. I have more experience with kidnapping negotiations."

"And I have more experience dealing with drug lords and their minions. We've got his agreement to keep this a simple exchange. All the diamonds are GemPrinted. We want Campinera to take possession. Don't over-complicate it."

Before the pissing contest got out of control I said, "Look, Katie is in danger and Hilly may be hurt. Put aside the egos and move out. The weather's not getting any better."

A gust of wind rocked the boat, even in the shelter of the marina, reinforcing my point. Vicky,

Hawk and I will land at the cay. I'll wear a wireless earbud and throat mike. Hawk will stay with the boat linked via his comm set. Dino and his two crew members, patched in to Hawk by marine radio, will remain in the deep channel. I could see he didn't like it, but he was outmatched by two large ex-SEALs and one determined DEA agent, armed and dangerous all. We headed out without further delay.

~~~

HIGH WINDS CHURNED up fifteen foot waves that raced in from the southeast. The roller-coaster ride from Marathon to Cay Sal Bank took a full two hours. It was 1145 when Vicky and I entered the tower. Carlos was already there. There were two armed thugs behind him, bookends on either side of Katie. Her wrists were bound with a zip tie. Hilly lay motionless on the floor in front of them a bandage wrapped around his head.

I called out to Katie, "Are you okay? What happened?"

Katie started to answer, but Carlos raised a hand and she stifled. "Your sister has been instructed to keep silent till we conclude our business. Be assured that she has been treated well. Her husband is not so good. But it is his own fault. He tried to resist. A futile effort."

Vicky stepped closer, within ten feet. I stayed a foot behind and to her right. Close enough to dive at Carlos, apply a choke hold and trade his release for my sister's if the diamond-swap gets screwed up. Carlos is no fool. He moved back two paces, closer to Hilly. An awkward arrangement so I cooled it and let Vicky speak.

"I can see that you are an intelligent gentleman, Carlos. Your boss will be pleased. Here are the diamonds."

She held up the satchel. It contained nine pouches like the one we left with Jorge yesterday. Eight contained eighty-nine diamonds, the ninth had eighty-eight. A total of eight hundred. We hoped Carlos would take our word that each pouch contained one hundred.

Carlos took the satchel, walked behind his bodyguards and said to Vicky, "Forgive me for not trusting a beautiful woman, but experience has taught me to be cautious." He opened a case on the floor. "We have many tools to improve the productivity of our business. This pill counter will count 500 per minute." He flashed perfect white teeth at Vicky. "After all, diamonds are just very expensive pills, yes?"

So much for our plan to fool him. In less than two minutes it could get ugly.

Carlos squinted at the counter as he poured each bag of diamonds into the loading tray. After a few loaded, he looked up from the readout and said, "You are sure all of our diamonds are here? It will be most unfortunate if that is not the case." He continued to load more. I looked at Vicky. We needed to disarm the body guards . . . now.

Hilly moaned and started to get up. Just the distraction we needed. With surprising quickness, Vicky lunged at the thug on the left. Hilly must have been faking the severity of his injury because he spun his legs like a whirligig beetle, tripping the guard, making Vicky's task easier. She used the momentum of the guard's downward fall to drive his head onto the cement floor, and knocked him out.

Not one to be left out, Katie pivoted and drove her knee into the other guard's groin then stepped toward Carlos. I wasted no time kick diving at the groaning guard. My boot connected with the back of his head as he doubled over from Katie's knee thrust. He staggered but held on to his gun. The guy must have brass balls and a cement head.

Carlos took a knife from the pill counter case, slammed the lid closed, and slung the strap over his shoulder. He held the blade to Katie's throat, pulling her along with him as he backed out the door. He shouted to the bodyguard that was still armed, "There are only eight hundred diamonds. Jorge will not be happy. Don't let them follow."

Vicky and I held our hands up. I spoke into my comm mike, "Hawk, do you copy? Carlos has the diamonds but won't release Katie. His guard has us at gunpoint and Carlos is getting away." I listened to the crackling static in my earpiece.

"Roger that, CJ. Sounds like the swap is totally FUBAR. The breakers are huge out here. I'm not at the dock. I'll be five minutes at least."

The armed guard tore the mike from my collar and threatened to shoot. I looked out the open window behind him and saw Hawk navigating around the rocks in heavy surf a few hundred yards out. Carlos still had Katie in tow and worked his way down a path to a second landing opposite where Hawk was headed. I caught a glimpse of another boat. It was a Cigarette, and it was purple.

~~~

MY MIKE WAS OUT, Hawk will be coming in blind. Vicky and I kept talking to the gunman to keep his attention away from the doorway.

Vicky said, "Your boss left you and your partner behind. Do you really think he'll send someone back for you?"

I added, "You know the drill, *hombre*. It's time to think about your future. Give me the gun."

He shook his head and backed up a few steps to check on his unconscious partner.

Right on cue, Hawk poked his head in the doorway. The gunman was still looking down at his partner. The howling wind helped mask Hawk's movement as he put a choke hold on the guard. After zip-tying the two thugs around a support column the four of us, with Vicky in front and Hilly wobbling between me and Hawk, descended the path to my boat.

The waves were bouncing it around but Hawk had strung all available fenders over the gunwales. *Too Fast For U* was safe and ready to go. But we wouldn't be chasing Carlos' fast boat. It was right there, tied to the dock, pounding her hull against the rocks—and it wasn't purple.

16

THE CHASE

I RADIOED DINO before I came in to get you," Hawk said as he glanced at the Cigarette and jumped on board *Too Fast For U*. "He said he'd try to intercept Carlos. Isn't this Carlos' boat?"

We looked to the southwest at a purple Cigarette kicking up a rooster tail as she pounded through fifteen foot waves a half mile out.

Vicky said, "Carlos must be on that boat."

Hawk said, "The Cigarette's fast. We need to go now if we want to catch him."

We joined the chase with Hawk at the helm. Carlos had to be stopped before he reached the Nicholas Channel. Cuban gunboats patrol the northern coast east of Havana. Closest Cuban coastline is just thirty miles due south across the Channel, straight through their patrol lanes.

Fourteen-hundred horses strained as they propelled us from wave-top to wave-top. Looking east at the shallows over the bank, wave height reached nearly twenty feet with many breaking into a frothy curl.

There's a coral reef protecting Cay Sal Bank. We stayed in deeper water at the western edge where the bottom plunged a thousand feet down Cay Sal Wall. Too deep for even the biggest waves to break. Hawk pushed to nearly full throttle. *Too Fast* didn't mind but the rest of us were feeling every bone-jarring jolt each time we flew over the top of a big roller and slammed onto the back of the next. We narrowed their lead to less than a quarter mile.

Their heading shifted toward the coral heads of Rompidas. I shouted to Hawk, "Stay out here. With luck the coral will bend their props, then we'll move in." The draft of my boat is a foot less than the Cigarette's deep V-hull design. We'll need it to get through.

As we closed in I read the name on the transom — *Purple People Eater* — confirming Dino's treachery. Their boat lurched as it powered into a trough, then surged through the coral head unscathed. In just a few minutes they will pass the twenty-fourth parallel and enter what Cuba considers her territory.

Hawk slammed the throttles full forward. We flew past the coral head. Automatic weapons fire emerged from the Cigarette's aft deck. The first volley missed us completely. Carlos was a poor shot and Dino wasn't much better, especially from a moving boat. A third shooter, one of Dino's deck hands, took his time. A bullet struck our windshield but we pressed forward.

Two more boats approached from the south. They were slower than the Cigarette but much larger and were painted drab gray. Cuban gunboats. *Purple People Eater* headed straight for the gap between them. They did not interfere. Another bribe did its job. After Carlos and company passed through, the gunboats closed the gap and fired a few fifty caliber rounds over our heads. Outgunned, we turned back.

With a following sea, our ride in *Too Fast* back to Marathon was a little smoother than the trip down but not by much. No diamonds. No Katie. Just Hilly. Time for plan B. Vicky was seething about Dino and his crew. She was on her sat-phone talking to Washington. Even FBI agents can be bought these days.

17

OPERATION KATE

VICKY ENTERED THE ROOM with photos from the National Reconnaissance Office. An NRO KH12 satellite spotted a Cigarette boat docked in the port of La Isabella, Cuba, a narrow peninsula on the northern coast just forty miles from Cay Sal Bank. Comparing sequential photos taken hourly, analysts determined the purple colored boat arrived yesterday afternoon between one and two o'clock. The viewing angle of the satellite was low enough to get a photo of the stern. The boat's name: *Purple People Eater*.

Infrared images showed hot engines, and confirmed the early afternoon arrival. After sunset, the geostationary KH12 also detected thermal signatures consistent with three live bodies in a dockside warehouse. It's got to be where Katie is being held. Hilly was in poor condition but still wanted to join the rescue. No way. We planned an underwater infiltration.

~~~

WE ARRIVED at first light, swimming the last mile underwater from the unmarked Zodiac we used to infiltrate Cuban waters. Hawk's friends on the CG cutter, *Mohawk*, unofficially dropped us in international waters. They didn't want to know our final destination. We left the inflatable adrift. The seas had calmed a bit since the storm so there was little wind. The Florida Current will take the featherlight boat east, away from our entry point. We plan to commandeer *Purple People Eater* for our exfiltration with Katie.

The eastern sky turned from deep red to gold when we surfaced next to the dock. The Cigarette was unoccupied and a dim light shone from the warehouse a hundred yards from our position. La Isabella is a tiny, sparsely populated port. No large ships, just a few small fishing boats moored along the narrow harbor channel.

Hawk took point, in stone-cold-SEAL attack mode. Katie was like a sister to him and, despite our plan to avoid lethal contact, he would kill to get her free if it became necessary. That makes two of us. We took a quick look in the Cigarette — keys in the ignition and full fuel tanks. Someone planned a quick getaway. How thoughtful. Ours was a risky plan with so many gunboats patrolling the coast east of Havana, but the element of surprise and low light conditions will improve our chances of success. The breakaway speed of the Cigarette will help. First, we need to locate Katie.

As we approached the warehouse a man stepped out the front door and spotted us. One of Bachero's crew. He turned to go back in but Hawk lunged after him, delivering a kick to the back of the head that sent him to dreamland. Hawk stuffed a rag in his mouth and zip-tied wrists to ankles from the back.

The cinderblock building had one window on the side facing us. A turkey peek revealed two people; one prone, one sitting slumped over, hands behind, bound at the wrists. I signaled to Hawk.

On three, we busted through the door. Carlos woke to find a gun barrel pressed to his head. Katie was awake and smiling at me. Bachero was nowhere in sight.

"I underestimated the resources at your disposal, Señor Charley. How did you find us so quickly?" The unflappable Carlos spirited a broad grin.

I ignored the stupid question and surveyed the room. The pill counter case was sticking out from under his cot. "I see you still have the diamonds with you."

"Of course. I would not dare deliver less than the full amount to my boss. You have seen his handiwork. You would have heard from me later today to get the last one hundred, but you have saved me the trouble. Now that you are here, I would appreciate receipt of the gems. In return, I will ensure your safe departure from Cuba."

This guy's got balls. A SIG Sauer pistol pressed to his temple and he's acting like he's in charge. "Always negotiating, Carlos. Have you been smoking the local weed? What makes you think we need your help?"

"Why not take advantage of my offer? What do you have to lose?"

"I don't have the rest of the diamonds."

Carlos' smile disappeared. "That is most unfortunate. Most unfortunate for all of us. Campinera is not very understanding when it comes to money."

Hawk motioned for me to look out the front window. There were several men in Cuban military uniforms gathering. I turned to Carlos, "All right, Carlos. Let's all walk to the fast boat together and get the hell off this island." I wasn't sure who the prisoners were with this arrangement but getting away from Castro's army was my first priority.

We stepped outside, Carlos shielded us as I held my pistol at the back of his head. Katie grabbed the diamonds. The soldiers raised their weapons but moved aside as we shuffled past. Carlos shook his head when one of the soldiers fired a warning shot in the air. They broke ranks after we boarded the boat.

Hawk cranked the engines and readied for a fast exit while Katie released the lines. I kept my pistol against Carlos' head, clearly visible to the soldiers as we raced through the harbor to the open channel. We got through without further resistance. Unless you count dodging several dozen fifty-caliber rounds aimed by one of Cuba's finest patrol boat gunners. Fortunately, he wasn't a very good shot and we were a rapidly accelerating target. I had tied Carlos to the aft cleat, an open area exposed to the wind and spray. He turned white when a few tracer rounds flew overhead. Mr. Cool finally showed some fear.

The *Purple People Eater* showed us her sprinting ability. We topped ninety mph when the water smoothed out on the straits. Katie sat between Hawk and me in the heavily bolstered middle bucket seat near the helm. More comfortable than Carlos' seat. A rising swell from the east made our escape more like a roller-coaster ride back to Marathon. Apparently, Carlos didn't enjoy amusement parks.

18

PLEA BARGAIN

COVERED WITH HIS FINGERPRINTS, the case of diamonds connected Carlos to the drug payment. Juan Madera's murder was another matter. The absence of fingerprints on the body and the fishing chair weakened the U.S. Attorney's case. But drug dealing and kidnapping were serious crimes. Carlos needed to cooperate to avoid jail. Jorge Campinera was the more important target. Time to negotiate a plea bargain with Carlos.

Vicky leaned over a handcuffed Carlos. "Ready to do some serious time for running drugs, kidnapping and accessory to murder?"

"You want Campinera. I'm just a little fish."

"Still negotiating, Carlos?"

Carlos smiled. "What if I testify Jorge killed Juan? Will the Feds drop the kidnapping charge? And the murder-accessory charge? After all, I was just following his orders."

Vicky said, "Very generous of you, Carlos. Selfish, but generous. But I also want you to help me get closer to Jorge."

"How?"

"Call him and tell him you have all the diamonds and I want to take him up on the rain check from my last visit."

Carlos smirked. "Yes, I'm sure he would enjoy your company."

So it was agreed. Vicky will go with Carlos. During the visit, she hoped to record more incriminating comments from Jorge before pushing for an indictment. If all is successful, the charges against Carlos will go away.

~~~

VICKY AND I STOOD on either side of Carlos while he phoned Campinera. We made the call from Carlos' mobile using speakerphone to record both sides of the conversation.

Carlos said, "Good news, Jorge, we have the diamonds. Everything went according to your instructions."

"Did you eliminate the Hildebrands after you got the gems?"

Carlos frowned and looked away from my glare. "No, Jorge. They are back with Señor Manner."

"I told you to make sure the kidnapping would not come back on us. What happened?"

Carlos stammered, "There were too many of them. I was fortunate to get away with the diamonds."

"You are a fool, Carlos. Again, you have failed to follow orders. When will I receive the gems?"

"Day after tomorrow. The weather is still bad and the high seas make a trip from here to Miami quite difficult."

"Okay, Carlos. I will deal with Manner and the Hildebrands another way. I do not want to lose my diamonds again. Remember what happened to Juan Madera. My knife is still very sharp."

Carlos smiled, "Of course, Jorge. You're the boss. See you day after tomorrow." I poked Carlos and pointed at Vicky. Carlos continued, "I almost forgot, Jorge, you can expect Victoria Barnes as well as the diamonds. She was impressed with you on her first visit and would like to stay longer this time."

Jorge replied, "*Muy bueno*, Carlos. Please send my best regards to Victoria. Tell her I will have something very special for her."

"Yes sir. I'll do that."

I pressed the end call button. Vicky grabbed Carlos before I could strangle him and said, "What did Jorge mean, *eliminate the Hildebrands*?"

Carlos flushed. "My instructions were to kill them once I had the diamonds. Of course, things have changed."

"They certainly have. You better keep up the pretense, Carlos, or your bargain will dissolve."

I checked my anger. It's Campinera that is threatening me and my family. We've got to give Carlos some rope to help us nail his boss. Carlos must have read my thoughts. He smiled and said, "You can trust me."

Vicky smiled back, eyes narrowed, and said, "I don't trust you for a second, so watch it."

And Hawk and I plan to watch them both, in case things go wrong at the penthouse.

19

FAMILY REUNION

HILLY was more shaken by the kidnapping than my sister. Sure, he was the one with a bashed in skull and the stitches to prove it, but it was the near-loss of his new wife that affected him more. He wanted no more to do with the cartel people but Katie was out for payback and she vowed to get it. With Carlos in custody and a sting planned to bag the big guy, she bugged me for updates.

"Where's Vicky? You guys are going after Campinera soon, right?"

Hilly wrapped his arm around her and shook his head but said nothing.

I put my hands on her shoulders, looked her in the eye and said, "Cool it, Katie. The less you know the better. Don't worry, we'll snag the little twerp and Vicky's evidence will put him away for a long time, sooner than you think. Maybe he'll get the death penalty if the murder charge sticks."

Her eyes narrowed. "Okay, but sooner isn't soon enough."

"Until Vicky gives us the go ahead, we need to tread water, little sister. At least for another day. As soon as Hawk gets here, we'll cruise over to Key West and have lunch at The Hole. After what you and Hilly have been through, a little family reunion celebration is in order."

Hawk untied the lines and hopped aboard *Too Fast For U.* We cruised out of the marina and reached The Hole on Stock Island fifty minutes later. Its full name is The Hurricane Hole, one of my favorite dockside restaurants in Key West. There are two lagoons nearby, known as hurricane holes, ideal locations to moor your boat during a hurricane.

The Hole offers an unusual service. If you are a fisherman you can bring your catch in and have them cook it up. Blackened, fried, baked, corn crusted or buffalo style … whatever floats your boat. Chef Tyler is the best. I have a business arrangement with the owners to supply fresh catches from my outings on the straits. They pay a fair price for marlin, swordfish, shark, tuna and wahoo. A good supplement to my Navy pension.

It was time to appreciate family. Life is good here in paradise, but it can end in a heartbeat. I learned that during more than a hundred ops in Iraq and Afghanistan including a sortie in the Spin Ghar Mountains when I became a guest of the Taliban torture team. But Katie's abduction brought it closer to home. I wanted to spend some quality time with my sister and her healing husband.

I had no fish of my own this trip, so we ordered from the menu. Hawk and I sat facing the water. Katie and Hilly were seated opposite us, admiring the huge salt water tank of fish in the center of the restaurant. I looked out at the smooth water of the lagoon. A large dorsal fin rose above the surface about a hundred yards out. A tail fin trailed nearly twenty feet behind it.

Hawk saw it too and said, "Is that your pet shark *Jawselle*?"

"It sure looks like it, but what's that behind her?"

A sleek, all-black fast boat was entering the lagoon, cruising at idle speed, no wake. And no name or numbers! Two hooded men in black raised AK47's in our direction. I yelled gun, leaped up and pulled Katie to the floor behind a potted palm. A burst of automatic weapons-fire peppered the dock and found its way to the fish tank, exploding the glass, spilling ten-thousand gallons of water and a few hundred tropical fish. I peeked through the palm fronds and caught a glimpse of the black boat speeding out of the lagoon.

I looked around. Hilly was lying among a dozen flopping fish. He was covered with glass shards. A pool of red surrounded his head. He didn't move. I nudged Katie. She looked up and said, "Where's Hilly?"

I held her close and whispered, "Are you okay? I'm afraid Hilly was hit."

She tried to get up and stumbled on the wet floor. I helped her stand and led her to Hilly. She cradled his head in her arms, searching for the source of blood. The sirens announced the arrival of the local ambulance. Hilly's eyes were closed but I could feel a pulse. The EMTs checked his breathing and placed a compression bandage on the side of his head. It looked like a grazing bullet wound, very close to the stitches that sealed the Cuban rifle butt gash. Hilly's got a hard head. He'll pull through . . . I hope . . . for my sister's sake.

I expected Katie to freak out but she just stared, tears streaming down, mumbling softly into Hilly's ear. I'd seen that look before, when our dad was killed and his body was returned in a military transport. He was supposed to finish up his last assignment and retire to spend more time with us while we were still young. I was nine, Katie was thirteen. Little did we know that Mom would die in a car crash a year later. Not much family left now—just Katie and me. Hilly was a welcome addition and I hoped it stayed that way.

Another family reunion gone wildly off course. I said to Katie, "We'll do the sting tomorrow and make Campinera pay."

She climbed into the ambulance still holding Hilly's hand, looked back and said, "Be careful, little brother."

Hawk and I walked back to the dock. More trouble. *Too Fast* was listing to starboard. She caught a stray bullet. One more reason to nail Campinera to the wall.

20

DRUG LORD STING

FIVE MINUTES BEFORE noon, Vicky and Carlos entered the elevator to Jorge's penthouse suite. Carlos carried the satchel of diamonds. Hawk and I were already on the roof of the building, on the west side, above Jorge's windows that overlook Biscayne Bay. Vicky will try to record more evidence during her 'lunch' with Jorge. She was wired again, a detail not shared with Carlos, for obvious reasons. Hawk and I will remain on standby unless things got rough.

When we arrived on the roof, we found a shed with a small, two-man helicopter parked inside. No guards. Nobody at all. We hid in the shadow cast by the shed's overhanging roof.

I could hear every word Vicky said as well as anyone else speaking within fifteen feet of the button bug on her blouse. She could hear my signals and voice through an embedded ear plug. The elevator door chime sounded. I clicked my mike three times to signal Vicky that we were in place. She acknowledged by saying, "Behave like a gentleman, Carlos."

A familiar voice said, "Of course, Carlos is always a gentleman, Victoria." Jorge was waiting at the elevator, no doubt with his two muscle-bound guards on either side.

"I'm pleased that you have decided to return to visit me, *Vicky*." There was a twenty second silence, except for the sound of Vicky gasping, followed by her muffled shout.

Jorge sneered, "Your name *is* Vicky, isn't it? But your last name is not Barnes. No need to answer. I have many spies, including some of your own DEA colleagues and, of course, Señor Bachero. He just called and confirmed my suspicion about you. A shame, really. And I thought your interest in joining me for lunch was sincere. Let her speak, Ricky."

I heard Vicky clear her throat. In a calm voice, she said, "You must be misinformed, Jorge. I'm thrilled to come back to see you." She was stalling. Still trying to get him to talk into the bug. What a gutsy broad.

"If you prefer to keep up the pretense, Ms. *Borne*, I will play along. You are too beautiful to treat badly, right Carlos?"

"Of course, Boss. I told you she was a Fed."

Damn. I knew we shouldn't have trusted Carlos.

I said to Hawk, "Sounds like Vicky is not in immediate danger. Let's hold back. See if she can get Jorge to open his mouth before we bust her out of there."

Vicky confirmed my assessment of the situation when she said, "Jorge, you misjudge me. I am tired of my job and would love to join you. Let's have lunch—alone—and see where it leads us."

I swear I could hear the drool dripping from Jorge's mouth as he said, "I do get lonely. Let us go onto the balcony. As you suggest … alone."

I looked at Hawk and said, "They're going to the balcony." We moved our position to the edge of the roof directly above them.

As soon as we refastened our rappel ropes I heard Vicky scream, "You better not let go of me, Jorge. I swear I'll cut your balls off."

A quick peek over the roof edge was all I needed to see Vicky hanging upside down by her ankles. The wiry old bastard held her over the railing and laughed as he called his minions. "Carlos, Ricky, Ramon, come here. This vixen is wearing a bug. Time for her to fly or die."

Hawk didn't need my signal. We leaped over the edge, rappelling twenty feet to the balcony railing. Boots versus chins — boots win every time. Our rappels were timed perfectly to intercept the baby Huey twins, Ricky and Ramon, as they rushed onto the balcony. Carlos grabbed the satchel of diamonds and headed for the door. Jorge let go of Vicky's ankles and trailed after him. Vicky grabbed the railing just in time to keep from falling fifty floors. She dangled with only a single handhold. Hawk and I were still dealing with the twins.

The rising whine of helicopter blades coming from the roof told me where Jorge and Carlos had gone. I looked up to see the chopper heading south.

Vicky shouted, "Will someone please help me?"

I finished off Ricky with a kick to his throat and reached over the railing for Vicky, swinging her up. "Here you go, Vick. Our master sting operation got stung."

"No shit, Sherlock. Now what?" Vicky frowned.

Hawk finally subdued Ramon and zip-tied him to Ricky while they were still unconscious. His cell phone buzzed. "Hawk here. Affirmative. Yep, thanks."

"What's up, Hawk?"

"That was my Commander at Vaca Key. He just heard from the *Mowhawk* patrolling the straits. They spotted a small helicopter flying at five hundred feet, headed due south."

Vicky said, "I'm going to nail that little bastard. And add attempted murder to the list of charges."

"I suppose you'll want our help, Vick. There's no way you'll get official support to infiltrate Cuba, if that's where they went. Forget about extradition."

"You got that right, Charley. I'm counting on you guys. This has become personal. Bagging Jorge and that double-crossing *gentleman* is going to be sweet."

"Don't forget the dishwasher scumbag."

Vicky fumed. "Yeah, snagging Bachero will be a bonus. But Campinera is who I really want."

21

DEAD MAN TWO

THE COAST GUARD CUTTER docked at Vaca Key. Hawk, Vicky and I waited near the gangplank. We had gotten another call from the Station Commander this morning. Deputy Sheriff Walker had also been alerted. The body was found half way across the straits with a jagged stab wound in the chest and dozens of cuts on the neck and hands.

Two CG Seamen off-loaded the body bag to the ambulance gurney waiting dockside. Walker unzipped it for us to identify the body. The nose had been eaten off by some hungry fish. The silk shirt was the same design and color that Carlos Bandinera wore yesterday. There were several fingers missing but the right index was still there to get a print. Looks like Jorge did not appreciate Carlos' part in the sting.

Vicky spoke to Vince, "I need to get the body to Miami right away. The CSI unit that handled Juan Madera will look for matching knife marks."

I asked her, "Do you know where Jorge is hiding? I doubt he'll risk returning to Miami."

Vicky said, "I'm working on it. Best guess? He's still in Cuba."

22

COVERT CAPER

MY CELL PHONE buzzed. The caller I.D. showed Vicky Borne. Hope she's got good news. "Hey, Vick. You're up late."

"It's only ten o'clock, Charley. I just got a call from my NRO contact. The latest satellite scan has located Campinera."

"Let me guess. Cooba?"

"Good thing you aren't trying to make a living as a comedian."

"I'm still working on my delivery. So, am I right?"

MICHAEL MARNIER

"He's in La Isabella."

"Maybe I should get a place down there. I'm sure this call means you want Hawk and me to make another trip. Unofficially, of course."

"You're a sweetheart for offering, Charley. I'll owe you."

"*No problemo, Señorita.* I owe Campinera some payback for what he did to Katie. Hilly's still in ICU at Marathon hospital. Katie was supposed to call me, but I haven't heard from her since this morning."

"Give her my best when she does."

"Will do. Now what's your plan? Do we just cruise into the harbor and ask the Castro brothers to give up Jorge?"

"You realize I can't offer official support if you're caught, and it will be difficult to get you guys out."

"SEALs love danger. But seriously, since its Cuba we're talking about, we'll make it a simple snatch and grab. No lethal force unless we need it. Defensive weapons only, including some flash-bang grenades."

"And where did you get them, Mr. Macho SEAL?"

"Vince raided the sheriff's armory. The SWAT Team will never miss them. Hawk suggested we plan ahead. And now you're calling."

"Miami CSI matched the knife cuts and matched the corpse fingerprint to the print in Bandinera's file. The Coroner's report highlighted several defensive wounds on his palms. They also found bits of skin under the index fingernail."

"Jorge has a psycho's appetite for blood, enjoys cutting people up. Carlos must have put up a fight."

"They will try to match DNA with a sample taken from Campinera's penthouse. I'm sure Jorge's list of crimes will soon include Carlos' murder. The man has no heart." Vicky paused for a moment. "Charley, I want him dead or alive."

"I understand, Vick. After the hit at *The Hole*, Katie wants him fried in a chair. And I don't mean my fishing chair."

"I'll drive down to Marathon tonight. Wake up Hawk and get your stuff together. We need to move quickly. See you in two hours."

~~~

HAWK WAS HAVING a late meal at the Blue Parrot when I called him. I was still hungry myself, so I walked from D-dock to join him.

"Hey, bro. We've got some work to do. Hope you haven't had too much to drink."

"You know me, Charley. I'm still on call for Search and Rescue. The Guard frowns on flying under the influence."

"That's good to hear, cause we're gonna be swimming in about six hours."

I ordered a Mahi sandwich and an iced tea. It didn't take long to decide on a plan. Hawk and I will infiltrate SEAL style, just like the last visit. Exfiltration after snatching Jorge will not be by boat this time. With Jorge in tow, we needed to avoid prowling Cuban gunboats.

We will use a submersible sea sled to transport him beyond Cuban territorial waters. We bought the sled from Navy surplus last year for a search and salvage project on the Pourtalés Terrace. The sled covered a lot of area and provided the lift we needed. It fit in the dinghy bed on the forward deck of Hawk's boat.

"Vicky should be here from Miami in two hours. She can tend the helm and wait for us to snatch Jorge. I hope he can swim, or at least handle a rebreather unit."

Hawk nodded. "Yeah. No SCUBA. No bubbles."

~~~

AT O-FOUR-HUNDRED we released the submersible from the dinghy hoist cable and slipped over the side. Vicky will put out some fishing rods and troll in a wide circle until we return.

We chose a drop off point in international waters, twelve nautical miles north of La Isabella. The sea sled had a max speed of fifteen knots and a range of thirty nautical miles. The calm seas should make the round trip a cake walk.

Our route took us over a deep water section of the Nicholas Straits. Two thousand feet below our cruising depth lay the steep sloped bottom. The Deep Strait continued from there, more than a mile down to the west of our position. My fish friend, *Jawselle*, had risen from those depths to dine on my old boat.

The inbound ride was smooth and easy. One hour after our start we tied the sled to an underwater piling in the inner harbor.

The warehouse where Carlos held Katie two days ago was empty. Only a few buildings lay beyond the docks. A handful of run-down shacks leaning on one another along the main street. At the end, right where Vicky's G2 said it would be, a large two-level home stood out. It was well maintained from what we could see in the dim morning light. Campinera's safe house. We moved from shadow to shadow between the shacks, approaching from the east.

Two sentries leaned against the arched façade of the house. Dozing more than guarding the entrance. Hawk took one in a choke hold. I used the hilt of my SOG knife to knock out the other. This was too easy. I said to Hawk, "Something's not right."

Before I could say another word, the entire house lit up. A siren sounded and a dozen soldiers charged out of a building a hundred yards away.

"Too late to turn back, Hawk. Quick. Inside." Hawk took point as we climbed the stairway just inside the front door. We were armed with tasers but met no resistance until a bodyguard popped into the upstairs hallway. He wielded a machete, charging as he raised it over his head. Big mistake. Hawk side-stepped and jabbed his ribs with a karate punch. The guy doubled over exposing his neck for a second blow that sent him to the floor. He didn't get up.

Hawk zip-tied the guard. I took over point and headed for the door most likely leading to the master bedroom. Locked. One kick and a rolling entry brought me face-to-face with a second guard. He must have weighed three-hundred pounds. Armed with a machete like his buddy, he had the arms of a mountain gorilla. I know when I'm physically outmatched so I shot both tasers at once. Hit in the chest and abdomen, all three-hundred pounds collapsed at my feet. He vibrated like an electric razor skittering across the floor.

I looked around the room. No one else standing. Just a quivering bump in the middle of the king-sized bed. I yanked off the covers. "*Hola,* Jorge. Vicky sends her regards and an invitation to return to Miami. Of course, your room will have bars on the windows and doors."

Puffing out his puny chest he said, "I should have cut her up when I had the chance. As for you, there are soldiers surrounding this building. You and your friend will never escape alive."

Hawk came in behind me and said, "Gag this jackass, CJ. I found a laundry chute with a man-sized shaft. I'll bet it opens in the basement."

These old hacienda-style buildings have archaic plumbing, with sewers that empty into the harbor. Access would be in the sub level of the building.

"Let's go, Jorge. Time for a swim. Put this on." I tossed him a neoprene chicken vest with integral rebreather pack. He'll need the vest to hold off hypothermia since we'll be in open ocean water for a couple hours.

Jorge fumbled with the vest, seemed distracted. He looked at the floor near his nightstand. I spotted the satchel.

"What's this, Jorge? Could the diamonds still be in that bag?" He didn't answer. I cuffed him, scooped up the bag and shoved him into the hall.

Hawk took the chute first, followed by Jorge. As I entered the chute I looked back and saw the soldiers from the street burst into the hallway. I tossed a flash bang grenade and dove into the chute.

When I reached the lower level Hawk was already prodding Jorge toward the sewer. There was a man-sized grate in the floor. "We need to dive now, Hawk. The soldiers are on the upper level."

I grabbed the grate but it was stuck. No time to call maintenance. Shit.

Jorge grinned. Until Hawk smacked him on the forehead.

Need to think quick. I scanned the room and said to Hawk, "He doesn't deserve it but pull this slime into the corner behind that pile of cement bags and cover your eyes and ears."

I took another flash bang from my vest and jammed it in an opening on the edge of the grate, pulled the pin and ducked for cover.

The grate jumped free. Time to roll.

Hawk replaced the gag with the rebreather mouthpiece and pushed the drug lord into the hole. Jorge let out a muffled cry. I hope he can swim in shit.

The sewers in this old port were built three hundred years ago. They were used as escape routes by wealthy homeowners to avoid capture by pirates. The water and sludge flowed down the center. It was only knee deep, but I'd rather rebreathe my own air than inhale the stench in the sewer. Bad memories. Jorge's diving lesson will come later when we reach the harbor.

The sewer sloped below the water line at the inner harbor. Even with Jorge's reluctant dog paddling, it took only five minutes to reach the sled. Hawk tied Jorge to the center slot on the sled and we beat fins for deeper water. As the sled props picked up speed, we entered the Nicholas Channel.

Jorge seemed distressed. His breathing was erratic. I checked his mouthpiece and air supply. Tied to the center of the sea sled, he couldn't be tired. What's the big deal? I grabbed his head by the goggles, turning it so he could see my face. His eyes widened and he turned white. Started yelling into his mouthpiece, bubbles bursting from the sides. He was looking over my shoulder. I turned in time to see *Jawselle's* pearly whites flash past. A big grin that brought back fond memories. I wish I'd stashed a bottle of Gran Patron on the sled.

The shark didn't linger. One bump against the carbon fiber sled and she was gone. I guess she wasn't hungry. Jorge was still freaking out so I whacked him on the side of his head and drew my hand across my throat. He took the hint and settled down. We still had another hour's swim to the rendezvous point.

~~~

VICKY WORKED the dinghy winch like a longshoreman. She swung the sled on board with Jorge still shackled in and set it down in the dinghy bed. She hopped over the rear stabilizer and yanked off Jorge's mask. "Did you enjoy the swim?" He looked like he was going to puke. She said, "At least you're alive. More than we can say about Carlos."

Vicky mirandized Campinera while she frisked him. She pulled a pearl-handled switchblade from his front pocket and dropped it in an evidence bag. "Is this the knife you used to cut him?" Campinera's eyes widened but he said nothing. He looked down, shrugged, a smug smile on his face. Arrogant bastard. He deserved a beating for what he did to Katie and Hilly.

I had received an update on Hilly just before we left Marathon. After two days in a coma, he suffered a massive stroke. He didn't make it. The rifle butt blow was bad enough, but the bullet wound turned out to be more than a graze. Unfortunately, there is no evidence that incriminates Campinera. But I know he called for the hit. He'll get his, one way or another.

I handed the satchel of diamonds to Vicky. Evidence. I wonder if she'll give me a loan. Never mind. We tied down the sled, shackled Jorge to the front seat and headed back to Marathon. Our prisoner bounced around a little and puked on his soaked clothing a few times. That was his problem. Vicky had arranged to have a Deputy U.S. Marshal waiting at Vaca Key. He will transport Campinera via prisoner van to the Miami Federal Detention Center. What, no limo? Tough times ahead, Jorge.

23

TRIAL AND ERROR

THE MIAMI U.S. ATTORNEY issued an indictment for Campinera. Vicky had gathered a boatload of damnatory evidence, topped off with a recording of her close call with a fifty story balcony dive. The charges included drug trafficking, one count attempted and two counts of pre-meditated murder. Katie's personal testimony would add kidnapping.

The knife from Campinera's pocket contained traces of blood in the blade slot. Even a two hour ocean soak didn't remove the deposits.

There was enough to provide DNA matches to Juan Madera and Carlos Bandinera.

~~~

MORE THAN TWO HUNDRED people sat shoulder-to-shoulder in the Miami federal courtroom. Half of them were reporters hoping for a juicy story. Drugs, diamonds and murder, the stuff that creates sold-out special editions and bestseller books.

Assistant U.S. Attorney Eduardo Arnez strutted like a peacock to the jury box railing. He leaned into their space and smiled. His gleaming teeth were perfect and too white to be natural. He was first generation Cuban-American and a rising star in the Miami federal prosecutor world.

Unbeknown to the judge, jury and defense counsel, he had a personal conflict of interest with this case. Vicky and I had no clue either, until the end of the trial.

He extended scrawny arms, palms up and spoke in a strained, irritating voice. "Ladies and gentlemen of the jury, this trial will be brief and my opening remarks even more so. I know your time is valuable and Jorge Campinera is charged with serious crimes. Drug trafficking, possession of stolen diamonds, kidnapping conspiracy, and yes ladies and gentlemen, murder. It is my task to show you the evidence so that you will render an objective verdict. Once you have heard the facts, I am confident that you will find him guilty. With your help, justice will be served."

Sitting next to Vicky in the first row behind the prosecutor's table, I had a clear view of the jury. From the expressions on the jurors' faces, the AUSA wasn't scoring many points. He was coming across like an arrogant-jerk-know-it-all.

I glanced at Vicky. She wore a frown and glared at Arnez. She whispered to me, "He's overdoing it. If he blows this case, I'll kill him."

I mocked shock.

She said, "Just kidding."

I'm not so sure about that. Vicky had been working this case for nearly two years. She won't take failure lightly.

The AUSA concluded his opening remarks with a flutter of his arms and paraded back to his seat. A few jurors rolled their eyes. One shook her head. This was going to be a long trial. I'd rather be fishing.

Defense Attorney Harvey Michaels stood in front of the jury box, keeping a respectful distance from the railing. He took a deep breath and let out a sigh. What a drama queen, but judging from the jury's rapt attention, his shtick was working.

Michaels had a Perry Mason demeanor, a handsome face, impeccable light brown like-me-I'm-your-friend suit, and an air of confidence tempered with the right amount of humility. An endearing mix that produced hundreds of acquittals for his not-always-innocent clients. He was smooth, but not showy. His voice projected sincerity. The jury watched him closely, noticed every gesture, and listened to every word.

Vicky squirmed in her seat and punched me in the bicep.

"Ouch!" I stage-whispered in her ear. "It's early. Wait till they hear Katie's account of the abduction. And Hawk and I won't let you down when we testify about the body." She relaxed, but only a little. And then Arnez called her to the stand. He spent the better part of an hour with questions about the chain of evidence, the history of Campinera's record, all for the benefit of the jury.

The Defense did not seem concerned and passed on cross examination, but reserved the option for the future.

It was almost noon when the judge called a two hour recess. I had to run to keep up with Vicky as she raced out the door.

"Wait up, Vick. What's the rush?"

"I've got to get back to work. Find more dirt on Campinera before that rube Arnez blows the case completely. Maybe I should go see the U.S. Attorney. He must know Arnez is a jerk."

~~~

FIRST WITNESS for the prosecution in the afternoon session was yours truly. I walked to the witness stand, crossing in front of the jury box. As I settled in Jorge looked at me from his seat at the defense table, turning his eyes only. He kept his head facing the front of the courtroom. It was a cold dagger look. The whites of his eyes bulged. I could see the blood vessels in his right temple throb.

I am not easily intimidated. His visual threat only increased my desire to see him enjoy a life-ending jolt from Old Sparky at Florida State Prison or wherever they fry murderous scumbags convicted in Federal court. Of course, he could choose lethal injection—can you believe it's now the convict's choice? I bet his macho mentality would make him go for the lightning bolt up his butt into his brain. Going out with a flash.

After I was sworn in, AUSA Arnez said, "Mr. Manner, please tell the jury what you and your friend, Mr. Harold Handy, found in the Florida Straits six weeks ago."

I smiled my best boy-charm smile and told my story, from shark encounter to Coast Guard rescue to the return trip for my fishing chair when we found the flayed body of Juan Madera.

The men on the jury seemed to enjoy the part about Jawselle's preference for Gran Patron tequila. The women seemed to like my smile; the flayed body, not so much.

"And what did you do with the body?"

"Hawk radioed—"

"You mean Mr. Handy?"

"Yes sir. Mr. Handy radioed the station commander at Vaca Key for permission to haul the body aboard. We photographed it in the water first and used the dinghy winch to hoist body and chair together."

"And did you return directly to the Coast Guard Station?"

"Yes sir. Deputy Sheriff Walker was waiting with a CSI tech from Miami. They took possession of the body."

Arnez walked me through the discovery of the map, the phone call from Carlos, the visit from Vicky, my cooperation with law enforcement and the abduction of Katie and Hilly by Campinera's minions. The jury got it all in detail, except the part about Vicky's interrogation techniques. That's top secret.

Defense Attorney Michaels tried to smooth talk me into contradicting myself but it didn't work. He gave up after thirty minutes of cross-exam. Next up was Hawk. Same deal. The AUSA walked him through everything I said. Some of the jurors nodded off. Even an attempt by Michaels to trip up Hawk didn't get their attention. The judge noticed and adjourned for the day. It was past four o'clock.

Vicky had returned to the courtroom a few minutes before the adjournment. She invited me and Hawk to her place for drinks. Hawk begged off, said he wanted to check out the scene at South Beach.

Vicky must have found new evidence. She seemed less agitated about Arnez' bungling. Maybe she spoke with the U.S. Attorney. She'll tell me about it later.

We headed for her apartment on foot. The blast furnace typical of Miami late afternoons was moderate. Still, when we arrived it was clear a shower would be more desirable than a drink. We stripped and stepped into her custom Deniau Shower System, complete with six body sprays and ten inch overhead nozzle. Not that I noticed as she grabbed me by the mizzenmast and pulled me into the torrential deluge.

A most enjoyable afternoon delight followed by drinks an hour later. No interrogation this time but Vicky's vertical position technique was outstanding. We decided to order take-out Chinese and continued the 'meeting' through the rest of the evening.

~~~

VICKY WAS UP and dressed, standing at the kitchen counter when I poked my head out the bedroom doorway. It was 0600. The trial will resume at 0900.

"Eggs over easy, Charley?"

The smell of fresh brewed coffee perked me up. "I'm starving. You bet, Vick. If the invitation is open, I could find a reason to get away from Marathon and visit the big city more often."

"Don't get ahead of yourself. Last night was great, but I'm focused on my career right now."

"Just sayin' sweetheart. No problem. My only commitment these days is fishing, now that Campinera's in custody." Vicky smiled and shrugged. I'll take that as a maybe.

~~~

HAWK PACED outside the courtroom door when Vicky and I walked into the courthouse at five of nine. He looked worried, if that was possible. Stone cold stares were his forte.

"What's the problem, bro?" I asked.

"I checked in with my Commander this morning. There's new activity on the straits. Mostly drug runners. The chatter on marine radio suggests the word is out on Campinera's situation. The streets of South Beach are also humming. Rumors are flying about lost diamonds."

"That's Jorge's problem, not ours."

Hawk said, "I agree. Campinera's loss of control is his tough luck, but what about the rest of the diamonds? If there really are a thousand, some cartel stooge might find the last hundred."

Vicky said, "If it's Los Zetas, Jorge's absence will open the door for the Mexicans. I've got some

LZ members under surveillance. They're next on my hit list."

"Don't worry, Hawk. The last hundred diamonds are safe if Los Zetas can't catch wahoo." I checked the time. "We better get inside before the doors close."

~~~

KATIE WAS THE NEXT WITNESS, ready for battle. Fire flew from her eyes when she looked at Campinera on her way to the witness stand. The AUSA approached the stand after Katie was sworn in.

"Good morning, Mrs. Hildebrand. Have you recovered from your ordeal with Mr. Campinera's thugs?"

Defense counsel leaped to his feet. "Objection. Your Honor, the Prosecution is stating as fact what we only know as an unproven accusation about my client's involvement."

"Sustained. Mr. Arnez, please rephrase your question."

"Yes, Your Honor. Mrs. Hildebrand, are you well enough to describe to the jury what happened to you and your husband on December 13th?"

Katie took a theatrical swallow, wiped a tear and nodded. "Yes, I think so."

"I know this is difficult for you. Take your time."

"Horatio and I were in the second week of our honeymoon in Nassau. After a detour south to dive the Great Inagua reef, we headed home along the Old Bahama Channel. Two days out of Matthew Town, just past Cay Lobos, Cuban gunboats stopped us."

"You're sure they were Cuban? Not pirates?"

"Yes, but one of the men wasn't wearing a uniform."

Arnez took two photographs from the evidence table. "Is either one of these the man on the gunboat?"

Katie looked at both photos and nodded. "Yes, the one with eyes closed is a bit puffy and the nose is gone but I see the same scar on his left cheek." She looked at the second photo and said, "This one is the same man, just looks a little younger and not so pale."

Arnez turned to the judge and jury, waving the evidence bags. "These are exhibits A and B. The first is a headshot of the dead body found in the Straits of Florida a few hours after the defendant fled Miami in a helicopter. The dead man was with him and was very much alive. The second is a file photo of Mr. Carlos Bandinera, a known drug cartel lieutenant to Campinera and computer matched to the first photo."

Arnez turned back to Katie. "Please continue, Mrs. Hildebrand."

Katie looked at Campinera. His face remained stoic, except for his eyes. They bore into her. Katie is tough. She stared right back and said, "Horatio tried to keep the soldiers from boarding our boat. One of them struck him in the head with a rifle butt."

"Was he badly hurt?"

Katie continued to glare at Campinera. "At first, I thought he was dead. There was blood gushing from the side of his head. But he rolled over and opened his eyes. I grabbed a towel and wrapped it around his head." She looked at me from the stand. I felt like jumping the rail and pummeling Jorge. Katie must have sensed my rage. She gave me a brief smile and shook her head. Telling me to cool it.

Arnez got her attention. "Then what happened?"

"We were towed to a port south of our location and held in a warehouse on the docks."

"Did Mr. Bandinera stay with you?"

"For a few hours. He left that afternoon and came back the next day."

"Did anyone else visit?"

Katie sent an angry look at Campinera. "Yes, there was a second man, a little short, wiry man, much older. He rushed in a few hours after the first man left."

"Do you see him in this courtroom?"

"Yes, he is sitting ten feet from me. His face is unforgettable."

"For the jury and court record, please point to him."

Katie pointed at Campinera. He smiled and winked. What a jerk. The courtroom gallery buzzed. The Judge gaveled for silence.

"Did Mr. Campinera say anything to you and your husband?"

"He said we would not be harmed if my brother gave him the diamonds."

"What diamonds?"

"My brother and his friend found a map stashed in his fishing chair when they recovered it from the straits. Apparently, the man they found in the chair had hidden it before he died."

Defense Attorney Michaels leaped to his feet. "Objection, the witness is speculating. Her statements are based on hearsay."

Arnez said, "Your Honor, previous testimony by Mr. Charles Manner is consistent with what Mrs. Hildebrand stated. The evidence that we will present proves Mrs. Hildebrand's understanding is accurate. I beg the court's indulgence and patience."

The judge said, "Objection overruled. Please continue Mr. Arnez."

"How do you know about the map?"

"Charley told me about it after he and Hawk rescued me."

Arnez walked Katie through the rest of her story, leaving out the shooting at The Hole that ended with Hilly fatally injured.

Arnez wrapped it up. "Thank you for your testimony, Mrs. Hildebrand. I have no further questions."

The judge looked at the defense table. Michaels walked up to Katie, a wide smile on his face and said, "Mrs. Hildebrand, why would Mr. Campinera want to kidnap you and your husband?"

Katie looked startled, hesitated and said, "I guess you'll have to ask him. All I know is he showed up in the warehouse where Carlos brought us. He said we wouldn't be harmed if my brother brought him some diamonds." Katie looked at Jorge who was trying to avoid eye contact. "He certainly acted like the boss."

Michaels frowned. I guess he thought Katie was easily rattled. Not goin' to happen, bro.

"What were you and your husband doing in Cuban waters?"

"We weren't in Cuban waters according to our GPS."

"So you say."

Katie's face reddened and her nostrils flared. Watch out bro, she's about to knock you down. She said, "The GPS unit on our sailboat has waypoint monitoring. There is a record of our route stored in memory. Check it out." She was in full attack mode. "And why don't you ask me what happened to my husband? I'll tell you why. Because Mr. Campinera had him killed a week ago so he couldn't testify. Too bad his men missed me and my brother when they shot at us."

Before Katie said another word, Michaels made a fast retreat to his table. "No more questions, Your Honor."

The judge looked at Katie, admonished her for the outburst and instructed the jury to disregard her last statement. But we all know you can't un-say what was said. You go, Katie. That's my sister.

I looked at Vicky. "This is too easy."

She frowned and said, "It's what we don't know that concerns me. Arnez is a jerk and Michaels is too smooth. Something's wrong."

And so the trial went on for the next week with more witnesses and evidence submissions. Hilly's death wasn't mentioned again. It prevented testimony to corroborate Katie's but her 'disregarded' statement took care of it. Arnez was an arrogant ass but his staff and the evidence Vicky provided, including taped conversations with Jorge, made his case look pretty good.

On the afternoon of the seventh day the jury shuffled from the courtroom to deliberate. Michaels' closing argument was eloquent and appeared to impress some jurors. AUSA Arnez couldn't control his offensive demeanor and may have undone a lot of the good work he'd managed so far. Vicky wasn't too happy. Always willing to help, I volunteered for one more interrogation session at her apartment before leaving for Marathon.

24

VOLATILE VERDICT

THE JURY WAS STILL OUT one week after the trial. The bullet holes in *Too Fast* were repaired so Hawk and I went fishing. Vicky had turned down my invitation to join us. Said she had some urgent business with another drug bust. All work and no play has made her grouchy. I suppose the Campinera case is the real cause. We'll just have to wait for the verdict.

~~~

THE COURTROOM WAS STUFFED like a Bahamian pig. The jury had not entered yet but Campinera sat in the defendant's seat scanning the crowd. He saw me and smiled. I sat between Hawk and Katie. Vicky still hadn't shown up. We had not heard from her since Hawk and I went fishing.

I felt a tap on my shoulder. I turned to find AUSA Arnez standing in the aisle. He motioned for me to follow him outside.

When we reached the hallway he said, "I thought you should know before court convenes. Bad news. It's about Vicky."

"What's bad about it?"

Arnez stared at the floor. "She's dead."

I swallowed hard, took a deep breath, and looked Arnez in the eye. "What happened?"

He looked away and said, "She was called into a drug bust in South Beach. The lead came through Dino Bachero's unit. It was a trap and Vicky was shot in the back of the head."

I felt my blood pressure rise, did a slow count to ten and grabbed his shoulders. "Are you sure?"

"I got a call early this morning."

I looked at the courtroom door. "Campinera's people involved?"

Arnez continued avoiding eye contact. He shrugged loose, gathered himself and said,

"Campinera will appeal if the verdict is guilty. He's eliminating obstacles in advance."

"Like the attack in Key West?"

Arnez said, "We can't prove it, but we believe Campinera contracted the hit. Watch your back, Charley. Let's go in to hear the verdict."

I shook my head while my insides burned with anger. I stayed in the hall for a bit. *Vicky's dead? No... I don't believe it. There's more going on here and I'll find out what it is.*

~~~

JUDGE RODNEY SIMONS strode into the courtroom and plopped into his chair, motioning all to be seated. Defense Attorney Michaels remained standing and said, "Your Honor, I have just received some information about the Assistant U.S. Attorney that you should hear before continuing this trial."

The judge gave Michaels a stern look. "This is highly irregular, Counselor. The jury has reached a verdict and will enter my courtroom as soon as I call them. It better be good."

"Oh, it's good, Your Honor. Mr. Arnez has outstanding debts owed my client. A conflict of interest that prevents Mr. Campinera from receiving a fair trial."

Arnez face turned crimson. Judge Simons glared at both attorneys and said, "Counselors, please approach the bench."

I was seated in the first row behind the prosecution team, close enough to hear the judge scolding the men.

Judge Simons said, "Mr. Michaels, I assume your information can be substantiated."

"Yes, Your Honor."

The judge fumed. "Why the hell didn't you make this court aware of it sooner?"

"My client only told me about Mr. Arnez' debt a few minutes ago. His business manager brought documents with Mr. Arnez' signature on them. He owes my client more than nine hundred thousand dollars for gambling debts."

The judge looked at Arnez, who was sweating visibly. Arnez didn't say a word.

Judge Simons grabbed his gavel and suddenly stood. I thought he was going to hit Arnez on the head but he slammed it on the bench and declared a fifteen minute recess. He ordered the attorneys to follow him to his chambers. The courtroom buzzed. I looked at Katie and Hawk. This is not good. Vicky's been killed and Arnez is fucking up the trial. Could it have been on purpose?

Katie said, "Why didn't Arnez excuse himself? He must have known it would come out at some point."

I shook my head. "It was deliberate. Campinera got to him. Best insurance drug money can buy."

Ten minutes later, the judge returned to the courtroom. He hammered his gavel and said, "I am not happy about the situation but I have no choice. I am declaring a mistrial. The prosecutor has failed to recuse himself and withheld information about a conflict of interest."

The courtroom erupted. Reporters streamed down the aisle to alert their editors. Everyone was talking at once.

Judge Simons pounded his gavel for order and said, "The defendant is free to go after posting bail of one million dollars. The indictment still holds. A different prosecutor will be assigned and a new trial scheduled as soon as possible. Mr. Campinera, you must remain in Miami. I will release you with that understanding."

Defense Attorney Michaels said, "My client is innocent of these charges and will comply with the wishes of the court, Your Honor."

A stunned look shone on everyone's face except for the smirk on Jorge's. He looked at me and pointed a finger, like a gun, and winked. I saw Arnez make eye contact with Jorge for a second. Jorge waved.

I said to Hawk and Katie, "We have work to do. My bet is Campinera walks, permanently. Posting a bail bond won't be a problem for him."

Katie dug her nails into my forearm and looked at the judge heading for his chambers. "Judge Simons is naïve if he thinks Jorge will stick around for a retrial."

25

BREAK TIME

NONE OF THE EVENTS during the past few weeks seemed real. I needed to clear my head. Hawk and I headed back to the Wall.

I slipped a Black Bart lure between two teaser bait-lines Hawk had set from the gunwale rocket tubes. Feeding out a few hundred feet of eighty pound line, I checked the drag on my reel and strapped into the fishing chair. With only two of us for crew, we kept it simple. Normally, five to seven baits are set in a pattern with outriggers to keep the lines from crossing. Too complicated. I needed to think.

Hawk looked back from the helm after setting our speed to eight knots. We headed northeast along the one hundred fathom mark above the Wall. "Hey CJ, think there's a diamond-stuffed wahoo down there?"

I swiveled the chair around to check out the sunrise off the starboard bow. "Not likely. I'm happy to cruise out here all day. Don't care if I get a strike. Just thankful to be alive. I need some quiet time to decide what to do about Campinera. You know he'll disappear."

Hawk nodded and gazed at the eastern horizon. God-rays pierced puffy clouds and lit up low patches of morning fog. Overhead, clear sky brightened from pre-dawn gray to cerulean. "It's a lot better out here than that shit hole in Afghanistan."

I cringed at the memory. It was my final tour, just two days to go when I was captured by the Taliban in the Khyber Pass. In a cave a hundred yards into the side of a Spin Ghar mountain in no-man's land between Afghanistan and Pakistan. Tortured, hog-tied and dropped into a ten foot hole filled with human excrement and piss. I struggled to keep my head up, to breathe the foul air. I was ready to give up when I saw a light spill over the edge of the opening above. Then I heard a familiar voice. "CJ…are you in there?" It was Hawk. He'd come back, looking for his SEAL team mate.

I shook my head to chase away the bad memory and looked at Hawk. "I owe you, bro. I could not have lasted much longer. The bastards pissed all over me before they left."

"No worries. You'd do the same for me. Leave no man behind, right bro?" He looked me in the eye. "Do you still get the dreams?"

The line snapped tight, almost ripping the rod from my hands as the chair spun around. The drop strap held fast and the reel smoked hot as line screamed out. I yelled over my shoulder, "Not any more, Hawk." I started cranking. "This is a big one. I hope it's not *Jawselle* again."

Before I could crank in another foot of line, the fish breached, shaking the lure violently until it broke free. The fish was a wahoo. Maybe *the* wahoo? I replaced the lure with some live bait.

We trolled for the rest of the morning. Didn't get even a nibble. I chilled in my chair. Thinking about how I get Campinera for what he did to my family and to my friend.

26

JAWS OF JUSTICE

CAMPINERA HAD VANISHED since the mistrial. What a surprise. Hawk just heard from the Coast Guard. They spotted a two hundred foot mega-yacht anchored south of Cay Sal. On the edge of Cuban territorial waters. The yacht's name is *Angelina*, registered to Campinera. The man has brass balls, hiding in plain sight. Is he inviting a showdown? He must know I'll be looking for him. No doubt he's fuming about the hundred million dollars in lost diamonds. I'm sure the DEA appreciates the ninety million dollar donation and the rest is swimming somewhere out in the straits.

The case had fallen apart. Without Vicky pushing, there were no new arrest warrants, no ongoing investigation. The U.S. Attorney had backed off for some reason. *Some* is likely another bribe. There's no evidence officially connecting the drug lord to Hilly's or Vicky's death, but I know better. I don't believe in coincidences. I've decided to make sure Campinera is either brought back to the States for a re-trial or has a fatal accident. The corruption rampant within the justice system leads me to favor the second option.

Campinera could leave anytime to any ocean on the planet in his yacht, so we had to form a plan and move fast. Slim chance the bureaucrats will request extradition, especially if Jorge stays in international waters. With ninety million dollars in diamonds in their slush fund and Jorge's penthouse locked up, the DEA is in no hurry to mount an offshore arrest. Not going to happen.

We loaded our underwater gear, two sea scooters, and weapons. Hawk punched in GPS coordinates his CG buddies gave him for the last known location of the *Angelina*. Once we find her, we'll proceed from below the surface.

We made a big show of loading up *Too Fast For U* at the marina dock. A full complement of big fish gear stuck out the rocket launcher tubes of my fish-fighting chair. We topped off the fuel tanks and cruised southward to my favorite fishing spot near the Wall. Just Katie, Hawk and me. Our real reason for the trip would remain a secret between the three of us.

Katie took the helm and said, "You boys relax, you have a long swim once we get close."

"Roger that," said Hawk as he sprawled on the rear bench seat.

Flat water and no wind, we reached the Bank in an hour, cast out lines and began trolling in a spiraling circle pattern along the edge of the Wall. Two miles to the southeast sat the *Angelina.* Sunrise still two hours away, I surveyed the situation with my night-vision binos. Didn't expect much activity at four in the morning but there were two sentries, one on the upper deck, the other near the stern.

Hawk stretched after waking from his nap and said, "Are you ready?"

I nodded and we both went into the cabin to suit up; wetsuits, rebreathers, knives, tasers and pistols. This sortie might be wet in more ways than one.

At 0445 we slipped over the side facing away from the *Angelina*. With the sea scooters it took only fifteen minutes to reach the mega-yacht. First order of business, we disabled the sentry posted near the aft gunwale. Easy peasy. He was leaning against a bulkhead, half asleep. Hawk put a full choke hold on him and eased him to the deck. Zip-tied and gagged, he would not be part of this fight.

We started for the upper deck but stopped when a radio squawked from the sentry's pocket. I grabbed the radio and mumbled some Spanish into it as Hawk and I made a beeline for the second sentry position two decks up.

The topside sentry was clambering down the stairs to the middle deck at the same time. He held a walkie talkie to his ear, not paying attention to the threat coming his way. Without breaking stride, Hawk arm-barred him in the larynx followed by a rabbit punch to the back of the neck. A quick zip-tie and gag left us with nothing but silence outside the main stateroom. A light came on inside.

Peeking in the stateroom porthole, I could see a man standing next to the lamp table. He spoke into a satellite phone. A dish antenna, aimed through an open ceiling hatch, sat on the table. He turned slightly. It wasn't Campinera. *Shit*. I looked at Hawk and mouthed, *"Where is he?"*

Before we could search the rest of the upper deck we heard the drumbeat of helicopter blades. Approaching from the south, it landed on the helipad located at the stern of the *Angelina*. The flood lights on the pad lit up the face of the pilot as he unstrapped and exited the chopper.

Hawk saw him first. "There's your answer."

Jorge must have had a late dinner with the Castro brothers. We flattened on the deck in the shadow of the aft bulkhead. Jorge's man in the stateroom came out to meet his boss. They shook hands and went back inside.

I peeked in the open porthole and saw Jorge standing next to his bed, reaching into the nightstand drawer. It looked like a pistol. I motioned to Hawk — gun — and then we kicked the door in, tasered the man next to Jorge and shut the door behind us.

"Hold it right there, Jorge."

He looked bemused. "Why it's my favorite SEAL friends playing black ops patrol. What do you want?"

"What do you think, Jorge? We want to take you for a swim. Leave the gun in the drawer and lie down on the floor."

Hawk moved in to zip-tie the drug lord and his tasered bodyguard. As he stood back up, the door to an adjacent stateroom burst open. Dino Bachero rushed in with pistol drawn. Instinctively, Hawk's SEAL training took over. In one motion, he slipped his SOG knife from its scabbard and flung it, center mass, at the threat. The knife sunk deep into Dino's chest. End of threat. A death too quick if you ask me.

"Time to go, Hawk." He nodded and retrieved his knife. We were never here.

Odd that Campinera had only two sentries and one bodyguard besides the dishwasher on board. In case Jorge had Cuban gunboats escorting, we kept to our underwater exit plan. We dragged Campinera over the side to our sea scooters. There were spare air tanks mounted on each. We strapped one onto Campinera and stuffed a regulator in his mouth. We had our rebreathers but Jorge's SCUBA unit trailed bubbles behind us. Not a problem. Everyone on board was zip-tied or dead. Although the bubbles might attract a few fish. Twenty minutes later we arrived off the port gunwale of *Too Fast For U.*

Katie slid the throttles to neutral and jumped in front of Campinera as he flopped onto the deck like a hooked mackerel. She slapped him, knocking out the SCUBA mouthpiece. "You killed my husband, bastard."

Campinera rubbed his cheek and smiled. "Nothing personal my dear. It was necessary to silence his testimony. Unfortunately my men did not get you and your brother, too."

Katie fumed at hearing Campinera's admission of guilt. She was about to say something but stopped to look over the drug lord's shoulder. She pointed and we all turned. The early morning light was still weak but I could see a large dorsal fin moving toward us.

Before I could say a word, Katie took a step toward Campinera, who had stood up in defiance. She did not touch him but he still fell backward and tumbled over the gunwale.

Cuffed with zip ties, he struggled to keep afloat and yelled, "Help. I can't swim."

Katie smiled. "You won't need to swim."

It took only a second. The shark lifted Campinera by his legs, shook him once or twice before severing his limbs from his torso. Campinera's scream was cut short. *Jawselle* scooped up the pieces, looked up at me and I swear she winked. Can sharks wink? I snapped a salute. *Jawselle* flashed her teeth with an open-mouthed grin, dove deep and never looked back. I'm sure we'll see each other again.

Katie teared up and kissed me on the cheek. She took one last look at the spot where the shark executed Campinera then returned to the helm.

Not another word was spoken during the trip back to Marathon. Justice served naturally, celebrated silently. It didn't bring back Vicky or Hilly, but it still felt good. And I'm not convinced Vicky is dead.

27

SEARCH FOR TRUTH

FORMER AUSA Arnez slumped in the booth at the back of Joe's Stone Crab restaurant. He looked away as I walked up to him. The peacock demeanor was gone. A suspended license and possible disbarment will do that to a career prosecutor. It must be humiliating, especially given the circumstances that caused his rise to stall. I'm surprised Arnez agreed to meet. I guess he's got nothing to lose at this point. Unless Campinera still expects him to pay back the loan.

Oh yeah, the mistrial was payment and Arnez doesn't know Jorge sleeps with the fishes.

I decided to take the high road, set aside my extreme dislike for the scumbag. With Carlos, Campinera and Bachero all dead, he was my only lead to find out what happened to Vicky. I sat across from him. "Hello, Eduardo. Thanks for the meet-up. I'm guessing your presence means the drug cartel is through with you."

He gave a furtive look out to the street. "My life's a mess, no one answers my calls. Campinera has disappeared. I don't need more grief."

"Well, I won't keep you long. I want you to tell me again about Vicky's death. How did you find out?"

Arnez looked away and mumbled, "I got a call from one of Jorge's people. He said Vicky got ambushed during a bogus drug raid."

"And you believe this, why?"

"The call was a threat to make sure the trial would go their way. I hadn't seen or heard from Vicky for a few days. Unusual, considering the trial and all. He said I would be next if Jorge was found guilty."

"So you never saw the body?"

"No, it was a phone call, not a meeting."

"What else?"

"Look, Charley. I want to help you if I can. I need to clear my name and try to get my license back."

"Talk to me, Eduardo."

He eyed the people seated nearby and lowered his voice. "I heard that Los Zetas was involved, not the Cubans. Vicky was poking around their operation here in Miami."

Eduardo averted my hard look. "It doesn't add up, Eduardo. You said the call came from Campinera's crew. How do the Los Zetas fit in?"

"There's a love-hate thing between the Cuban and Mexican drug rings. Sometimes they work together if there is mutual benefit."

I remembered Vicky saying she had Los Zetas in her sights and planned to move on them after dealing with Campinera. "So you think she got ambushed by the Mexicans?"

"Yes, but what I think doesn't matter anymore."

"You'll get no sympathy from me, Eduardo. Do you know where the hit took place?"

"No, like I said, it was a phone call. Why don't you contact her boss at DEA?"

The scum bucket looked pathetic, but my gut told me he was telling the truth. I stood and placed my hand on the back of his neck, squeezing till he winced and said, "Then I'll be leaving you to your job hunting. Call me if you think of anything else."

~~~

HAWK STOOD by the window, peering through the blinds. Like a moray eel coiled in a hide-hole waiting for a meal to swim by. I hung up the phone and said, "Vicky's boss wasn't much help. He confirmed what Arnez said about Los Zetas but didn't have much more to offer. I managed to get the name of the guy they suspect is responsible—Jose Guizarro."

"Did he say where the dude might be?"

"His headquarters are located on Cozumel. He runs Los Zetas' Mexican and Central American operations."

"What's the connection to Campinera?"

"Vicky's boss said Guizarro wants to expand into the U.S. Southeast. He's actually American, born in California. The U.S. authorities have a five million dollar bounty on him for drug trafficking and money laundering. But the DEA is giving it a low priority. Guizarro has no outstanding warrants or convictions in Mexico, so the DEA is getting no cooperation from the *Federales*. ICE has him on their watch-list in case he dares a visit to the States."

"Sounds like the DEA has the same support the Border Patrol gets. I guess we're on our own."

"With all the corruption in law enforcement these days, I prefer it, Hawk."

Hawk smiled and said, "Cozumel, huh? Isn't their *Carnaval* festival this month? We could fly in and use the celebration as cover."

"Good idea, but I'd rather shoot across the Gulf in *Too Fast*. We can bring more gear that will give us better options, some firepower and a fast exit if we need it. We'll use the hidden compartment in the bow for our weapons."

28

REPTILIAN REDOUBT

FIERCE EYES blazing, the crocodile surged from the murky lagoon. Vicky's heartbeat quickened when the monster climbed the bank in front of her tiny island prison. It stopped inches from the rusty bars, opened its jaws and hissed, spraying a musky scent that gagged her. She moved to stifle a cough but the croc didn't change its threat pose. Just stared. Like the last time. She exhaled slowly, moved to the back of her cell and waited for it to go away.

She remembered little from the past few weeks. A drug bust gone bad. A hood thrown over her head. A long ride in a fast boat. She had been drugged, a spot on her upper arm was still sore. They carried her from the boat still hooded and hogtied. When she faked a retching fit they removed the hood. It was nighttime. They were in an SUV leaving a small marina. Where the hell was she? Who knows how far from Miami she had traveled? It was definitely south, and much warmer than Miami.

Vicky looked at the croc. As quickly as it had appeared, it turned and slithered back into the water, dropping beneath the surface without a sound. The same behavior since she arrived. A daily threat, a show of force to intimidate, to remind her who was in control. Vicky hated it when she lost control. The adrenaline rush subsiding, she still did not move and kept a watchful eye on the spot where the crocodile disappeared.

Jose Guizarro was playing mind games with her. Keeping her in isolation. No contact except his daily interrogation and the reptilian watch dog with halitosis threatening to crush the cage. Her strength sapped from lack of food and barely enough water to stay alive, she drifted off. *I'll sleep a little, get some rest. Need a clear head...must escape.*

~~~

A LOUD SPLASH jolted her awake. It came from the far edge of the lagoon. She could see the animal struggle in the water, squealing, a panicky cry for help. A piglet, maybe ten pounds, no more. The water swirled in the center of the pool. Mid-shriek, the pig disappeared, returning the lagoon to silence.

"You see what will happen to you if you do not cooperate?"

Vicky jumped. Still dazed from fitful sleep, she was distracted watching the little pig, did not see Guizarro cross the foot bridge to the island. He stood to one side of the cage, leering at her.

"Are you ready to cooperate?"

Vicky threw her head back. "I told you, I don't know anything about Jorge Campinera."

Guizarro reached into the cage and grabbed Vicky's hair. He pulled her against the rusted bars. "You are a stubborn woman. I'm losing patience."

Vicky gasped. "My people will be looking for me."

Guizarro scoffed, "You are in a cage, on a tiny island in the swamps of another island and a very large, very hungry crocodile wants you for lunch. No one will come for you. Your only hope is to answer my questions. Who are the DEA informants in Campinera's gang?"

Vicky remained defiant. She would not help Guizarro identify the moles and take over Campinera's territory. He'll kill her anyway. "I have nothing to say."

"Perhaps another day without food and water will change your mind. If not, then my pet will dine on more than pig." Guizarro crossed the footbridge as the croc returned to its watch. Bits of pork ribs were stuck to its front teeth. Looking back Guizarro said, "Don't even think about escape, Miss Borne. My pet will sleep while digesting the pig, so I will post a guard."

Vicky moved to the back of the cage, and watched the beast glide to the bottom of the lagoon, a few yards closer than before.

29

CARNAVAL DE COZUMEL

MID-FEBRUARY brings the annual *Carnaval de Cozumel*, one week before New Orleans' *Mardi Gras*. The celebration swells the population from eighty thousand to nearly a hundred thousand. Cozumel is a tiny island—thirty miles long, ten miles wide— mostly undeveloped scrub, with coastal lagoons and mangrove swamp. The majority of the locals live in the city of San Miguel, serving the tourists that arrive by cruise ship and airplane every winter.

More daring souls sail or motor to the island in their own boats. The influx of strangers will provide good cover.

With a flat sea, we cruised at seventy mph and made the trip from Marathon to Cozumel in five hours. We used an auxiliary fuel tank to extend the max cruise range of *Too Fast For U*. We had fifty gallons to spare when we idled into Caleta Marina on the south side of San Miguel at high noon.

After checking in with customs we refueled, rented a temporary slip and headed for the bars. Tomorrow is Fat Tuesday, the final day of *Carnaval*. Most of the inebriated revelers will gather at the curb for the processions along the downtown seafront, starting at the *placio*, down one side of Avenue de General Raphael Melgar to the Forum shops, and return on the other side of Melgar. I brought a photo of Vicky. We'll work the crowds. Maybe someone has seen her.

~~~

NO ONE in the last ten bars had seen Vicky. We'd bar-hopped the length of Melgar without a single lead. Some of the locals looked at us *gringos* and seemed nervous when shown the picture. We couldn't get past *¿has visto a esta mujer?* before they threw up their hands and rushed away. Just when I thought this wasn't such a good idea, a swarthy guy walked up to the bar and leaned over to look at the photo lying next to my drink. He looked at us and spoke softly, "Why do you want to find this woman?"

"She's a close friend. Have you seen her?"

"One hundred dollars, American."

I pulled a bill from my pocket and placed it on the bar. He reached for it. I grabbed his wrist and repeated, "Have you seen her?"

"*Si*, but it was a week ago."

"Where?"

The man looked around the bar. Then held out his other hand and rubbed his thumb against his fingers.

Hawk said, "He wants more money."

I had several hundred-dollar bills and offered one more. He shook his head. I added a second bill. He spoke again, barely audible above the noise of the *Carnaval* crowd.

"You must be careful. The man she was with is very powerful. I saw her in an SUV. They were driving out of town to the northern part of the island. The man yanked a hood off her head. That's what caught my attention."

"Any names?"

The guy rubbed his fingers and thumb again. I placed two more C-notes on the bar. He said, "Guizarro. A dangerous man." He scooped up the bills, turned and quickly left us without another word.

Hawk said, "I don't like it, CJ. Are we being set up?"

"What choice do we have? It's our only lead."

"What next?"

"Tonight, after dark, we rent a four-wheel drive and head north. I've already studied a map of the island. There are only a few roads, most on the coast end in swamp or lagoons."

~~~

THE AVENUE de General Raphael Melgar was nearly empty north of the parade route. We detoured a few times to get past some bottlenecks at the airport and the Cozumel Country Club. The GPS display showed a satellite view of the northern tip of the island. *Punta Norte.*

A mile past the country club we turned off Melgar before it curved east, away from *Punta Norte*. The hard surface road became rough, potholed dirt that tested the suspension of our rental and the fillings in my teeth.

"Better check our twenty."

Hawk pulled up Google Map on his cell phone and zoomed in to Cozumel, looking for a street view of the buildings. It amazes me how much of our world has been recorded by the probing eye of a digital camera. Government satellites are one thing, but private technology companies have taken it a step further. Even in remote areas, the digital eye has mapped the terrain, including street views.

Hawk said, "I think I found it. There's a large building behind a high fence." He looked out the window for a landmark. "Looks like we're about two miles from the gate. Do you plan to drive right up to it?"

"That's the quickest way to find out if we're in the right place. We're just *turistas* looking for a dive spot on the northern coast, right?"

The road narrowed to a single lane, elevated a few feet above mangrove swamp. Some areas opened to lagoons big enough for a small boat. The hacienda came into view. Before we reached the gate, two men armed with AK47's stepped in front of us. We stopped. One of the men walked up to the driver's side window.

"This is private property, Señor. You must turn around."

"Sorry, *hombre*. The guy at the marina said there's some great dive locations on the northern tip of the island. My buddy and I were trying to locate one."

The guard trained his AK at my face. "No, you must turn around. *Propriedad privada*."

I shifted to reverse and made a three-point turn while Hawk checked out the gate and looked for surveillance cameras.

Hawk said, "Let's come back after midnight. Maybe it will be by sea." He held his iPhone for me to see a Google Earth view. "The lagoon on the right side of the compound connects to the coast through a tidal creek."

~~~

THE SEA CHART of Cozumel lay on the table in the cabin of *Too Fast*. The chart included a detailed view of the inlets on the coast of *Punta Norte*. Hawk circled a large lagoon that fed into a small creek, ending at a deep water cut on the coast. He read the depth contour lines and traced a way in. "If we tilt up the outboards and use the trolling motors, we can get into the lagoon behind Guizarro's compound."

"We'll use our night vision scopes to navigate. If Vicky's not there, we don't want to make contact with anyone, especially the guys with AK47's."

~~~

WE WAITED till zero dark thirty to leave the marina. Fifteen minutes later we approached the cut in the rocky shoreline at *Punta Norte*. I killed the outboards and power tilted them out of the water while Hawk dropped the trolling motors into position. Silent running with night vision from here on out.

A gibbous moon provided some light through the vines and moss hanging from the mangroves along the creek bank. Like bearded sentries, standing on giant prop roots, the trees arched toward the seaward side of the island, guarding a fortress in the middle of nowhere. Boas dangled from the lowest branches, waiting for a feathered breakfast to cross their path. The channel narrowed. Aggressive kudzu reached across the gap, forming a tunnel-like passage.

Several pairs of green dots disturbed the smooth surface, the reflected moon-glow enhanced by our night vision goggles. American crocodile are known to live in these brackish waters. The largest specimens can be twenty feet from snout to tail-tip and weigh two thousand pounds. The eyes looked too close together to belong to a croc that big.

The creek divided in two. The channel widened to the right, through a break in the mangroves and opened into a large lagoon.

"This is the one," Hawk said as he checked the GPS app on his phone.

I reduced speed to drop our wake and continued into the lagoon. A faint light shone through the trees on the opposite bank a thousand feet from our position. I steered to starboard, through an arch of giant mangrove roots into a vine covered inlet, cut power to the motors and slid the bow silently onto mud exposed by a receding tide.

"Let's tie here and arm up."

I grabbed my SIG Sauer pistol, a coil of rope and a flash bang from the hidden compartment. Hawk reached for the Stoner SR-25 rifle with night vision scope. After ten paces I looked back where we stashed the boat. The dense foliage made it impossible to see even with the aid of night vision goggles. We continued along the edge of the lagoon toward the light, our footsteps silenced by the spongy carpet of swamp moss that smothered the ground near the lagoon.

Hawk took the lead and suddenly halted. He held up a closed fist and looked up. We waited a few seconds as a six foot boa slid off a branch in front of us, slithering after an early breakfast. A few minutes passed before the walled hacienda came into view, lit up by a single light mounted high on a pole in the middle of the compound. We circled around to the rear.

Fifty yards from our position, a lone sentry shuffled along a path leading away from the back entrance to the hacienda. We kept pace, remaining in the shadows of scrub trees bordering the path. The man stopped at a gate in a ten foot fence that surrounded another pool, separate from the lagoon we entered earlier.

Hawk placed a hand on my shoulder and whispered, "See that other *hombre* coming across the foot bridge? Looks like a guard change."

The surface of the moat rippled as the man crossed the bridge. He quickened his pace, opened the gate and nodded to his replacement. As the new guard walked across the bridge we moved in closer. There was a cage in the center of the small island. No vegetation hid the view of its occupant. No mistake, Vicky sat slumped on a chair. She was shackled by the ankles with a heavy chain looped through one of the bars.

I whispered to Hawk, "Any ideas on how we get through the gate and cross that bridge?"

Hawk was looking up at the trees surrounding the pool. Some large branches arched across forming a thin canopy. "You're lighter than me. Why don't you climb that tree and rappel onto the guard. I'll cover you from here."

Hawk set up in a sniper position resting the Stoner in the crook of a tree. With a little luck, we won't wake anyone in the hacienda. The silencer on the rifle should keep it that way if he needs to take out the guard before I get up the tree.

Half way up I was greeted by a fat boa curled around the branch I needed to fasten my rope. Her ten inch girth had a large bump a few feet past her head. She looked sleepy, digesting whatever caused the bulge.

I took a deep breath and slid off the branch to execute a hand-over-hand monkey bar maneuver. Got past without waking her or alerting the guard thirty feet below. I decided to keep things simple and drop onto the guard without rappel rope. If I aimed right, he would break my fall. As I released my grip on the branch, the rustle of leaves made the guard look up in time to welcome the heel of my boot with his nose.

Hawk sprinted to the bridge and took a defensive position facing the hacienda while I searched the guard for a key to the cage. Vicky stirred when I creaked open the door to her torture chamber. She was dazed but I could see she recognized me by the expression on her face.

"How did you know where to find me?" she slurred.

"I'll explain later, sweetheart. We need to get out of here, *pronto*."

There were two keys on the ring. I tried the second one on the padlocked chain. It worked, but the shackles were bolted onto Vicky's ankles so we'll have to leave the chain on till we get to the boat.

Half way across the foot bridge, the water rippled, followed by a set of teeth that rivaled *Jawselle's*. A huge croc leaped from the water and landed on the bridge, breaking it in half. The weight of the chain pulled Vicky under and the crocodile followed.

Hawk set his rifle down, unsheathed his SOG knife and dove after the croc. I dove after Vicky, grabbed her by the hair and pulled her across to the other bank.

Looking back we saw Hawk trapped in a death roll with the croc. He had an arm lock across its neck, riding the croc's back. I grabbed the rifle and took aim. Before I could get a shot, Hawk jammed his knife into the soft flesh at the base of the lower jaw. He plunged it deep, twisting it sharply to sever the spinal cord where it connects to the croc's tiny brain. Hawk rolled off and swam toward us, leaving the dead reptile for its mates' next meal.

Still no movement inside the hacienda. They must be on drugs. We retreated to the boat and slipped back toward the river mouth. Once we reached open water, we cranked up the Verados and made a beeline for the Keys. No point in sticking around. I'm sure the *Federales* are well bribed by Guizarro. Hawk took the helm while I stashed our weapons and dug out my tool box for a wrench. Vicky collapsed on the forward berth, alive but clearly exhausted.

~~~

VICKY OPENED HER EYES and smiled that smile at me. She'd been in and out of consciousness for the past forty-eight hours, waking briefly in a panic. Now she seemed calm and more like her old self— ready to kick ass.

"Charley, I think I'm back from my trip to hell. It is you, right?"

I took both her hands and kissed them softly. "It's me for sure, sweetheart. We've got some catching up to do."

"You first. What happened to Campinera and where is that scumbag Bachero?" Fire shot from her eyes. "You know I was set up."

"Yeah, I got the word from Arnez. He told me you were following up a lead that came from Bachero's department. Said you were dead."

Vicky shook her head. "Drugged, hooded and hog-tied but not dead." She forced a smile.

"Arnez also gave me the lead that brought Hawk and me to Cozumel. He's done as a prosecutor and will be lucky to get his license back."

Vicky sat up with a groan. "I guess I owe him for that. What do you mean *done as a prosecutor*?"

"That's right. You weren't there when the verdict came in. Before Judge Simons called the jury, Michaels dropped a bombshell. He showed the judge evidence that Arnez owed Jorge 900 G's in gambling debt. Simons declared a mistrial."

Vicky's eyes narrowed. "I told you something wasn't right."

"Here's some good news. Campinera's dead. You might say he had a swimming accident. A great white ate him for breakfast a week ago."

Vicky brightened. "That is good news. I hope the shark didn't get indigestion."

"You can scratch Dino Bachero off your payback list, too. He ran into a SOG knife when Hawk and I visited Campinera on his yacht. Long story, but it has a happy ending."

"Spare me the details for now, Charley, I'm so tired."

"Sure. Get some rest. I'll put the do-not-disturb sign out. No one else except Hawk and Katie knows you're here."

I gave Vicky a kiss and headed for the door. She called out in barely a whisper, "Charley?"

I turned and saw tears flowing down her cheeks. "Yeah?"

"Thanks. I really thought I was going to die in that cage or get eaten by the croc. When I'm back to one hundred percent, I want you to help me find Guizarro."

"Already on my list. Now, you rest."

~~~

IT TOOK A MONTH for Vicky to recover. Despite nearly starving her to death, Guizarro failed to learn anything about the DEA's plans to shut down his takeover of Campinera's territory. She didn't spill the names of DEA informants either. Her silence was the only reason she was still alive when Hawk and I found her. And none too soon. Vicky said Guizarro was losing patience and planned to feed her to the croc the next day.

Vick and I have been together 24/7 since we got back from Cozumel. She has not contacted her people at the DEA. Can't trust anyone, even her boss. Campinera and Carlos are dead but Guizarro deserves payback. Not yet. We need to sort out which side all the players are on, inside and outside the DEA and FBI.

30

GIFT FROM THE SEA

HAWK BACKED DOWN the boat while I wrestled with a big one, keeping my rod high so the fish wouldn't toss the hook. I sat in my lucky fish fighting chair securely mounted on *Too Fast For U's* aft deck. The fish was going to lose this battle. She breached the surface shaking the lure, trying to release the line. It was a wahoo... a big wahoo, close to a hundred pounds. I could taste the broiled filets drenched in melted butter topped with sliced almonds and a special hot sauce only Katie knows how to make. Her leaps were spectacular. The wahoo, not Katie. We came back to Cay Sal Bank near the Wall for marlin, but wahoo tastes even better.

"Keep that line tight, you squid."

I looked back at Hawk and grinned. I would have given him a middle finger salute but this fish was too ornery to land one-handed. Katie and Vicky came out of the cabin to witness my fabulous fish fighting ability.

It took close to an hour to get the fish on the deck. She nearly smoked my reel and spit out the hook making several leaps before running out of spunk.

Hawk put the throttles in neutral and came off the helm to grab the leader wire once I got her up to the port gunwale. He hauled her up. She was as long as he was tall. Something odd about her mouth. The marlin lure stuck out one side but the other side had a large hook protruding from the corner of her jaw.

I removed the hook with needle nose pliers. A steel leader was attached to the hook. I pulled on it. It was wrapped around the end of a rubber tube that had been crammed down her throat. Laying it on the deck, I cut it open and diamonds tumbled out. Big diamonds. I made a quick count … one hundred.

I looked up at Hawk. "Finders keepers?"

He grinned, "A ten million dollar gift from the sea. I sure would like to pay off the loan on my boat."

"Me too."

Hawk said, "I know a diamond dealer in Nassau."

Vicky just smiled. Katie went below to make more drinks. I stashed the gems and we headed east across the straits toward Bahama Bank. You might say today turned out to be a good day, but Hawk still scanned the horizon for signs of trouble. Out here on the straits, you never know when it will cross your path.

Wahoo!

THE END

REVIEWS

☆☆☆☆☆

A fine murderous romp. Fast boats, deadly gunplay, and a gorgeous wench

A fast paced and page turning romp filled with fast boats, gunfire, and close shaves both on, off, and under the sparkling waters of the Florida Straits. A thoroughly pissed off drug baron bites off more than he can chew as Charlie Manner and his rough tough mate decide to take him to the cleaners. Add a Great White Shark, some serious booze and a gorgeous wench to sweeten the lethal cocktail. If you liked John D Macdonald's Travis McGee stories you'll probably enjoy this. A book to be swallowed whole in one sitting, on a beach, or a train or plane journey. I was still reading it at 2 AM. A fine debut novel. I look forward to seeing the next.

☆☆☆☆

A fast-paced thriller with a larger-than-life hero

If you're a fan of larger-than-life heroes you'll enjoy *Trouble on the Straits*. Charley Manner is one of those guys who, by skill and rugged ingenuity, manages to get himself into a fix then out of it and live to tell the tale – more often than not in the bar afterwards. Imagine a cross between Clive Cussler's Dirk Pitt and James Bond's smart-lipped American cousin and you get the idea. Throw in a shark with a taste for tequila, a drugs baron who will stop at nothing to get his diamonds back, and a sexy DEA agent in a trench coat (and little else) and the stage is set for a contemporary yarn of derring-do on the high seas - or more accurately the Florida Straits. Gripping, enthralling and witty in equal measure – this has enough twists and turns to keep you turning the pages faster than a card sharp shuffling a deck (as Charley might say). My only reservation – I'd have liked to read more about the beautiful Florida Straits where the tale is set. Maybe the next in the sequel will set things straight.

Action and adventure…

A very entertaining read! Looking for a way to escape your daily routine? Grab a copy of Trouble on the Straits. Action abounds from the first page. The hero, brave and smart-mouthed, finds himself embroiled in dangerous situations involving a shark, a drug cartel, a pretty girl, and many lively characters. Charley Manner's adventures leave you breathless and asking for more. The narration is gripping, the style is flowing. Amusing and fast moving! Read and enjoy.

Meet a Great White shark with the personality of Moby Dick

Trouble on the Straits by Michael Marnier is a tight lines thriller, taut with danger, heroics, adventure and justice. It starts with a Great White shark with the personality of Moby Dick, and it races through a series of events that bring out the best in a Navy SEAL and the worst in a Cuban drug lord. The characters live through the author's imagination, full blown, larger than life, with love to spare and lives to live, and possibly lose. I recommend this thriller. Nice work.

If you enjoy nautical adventures spiced with tequila

If you enjoy nautical adventures spiced with tequila, thrills and danger then this story is for you. More a novella than a doorstep, you can romp through this riotous thriller in a weekend. Here is Charley, a former Navy SEAL lives in the languorous Florida Keys surrounded by good vet pals, spending most of his retirement fishing, drinking and telling tall tales. It was his fishing that lured him into trouble when a great white shark took revenge on Charley's hook & line, ate his boat (nearly) and landed him in the drink harnessed into his fishing chair armed only with his wits and a large bottle of tequila. He survived only to face more conflict from the Cubans when he discovered a map they wanted back. This is fast-paced written, with a wry smile: "Where did you learn this? – 'A fish told me'" - and charming metaphors: "We stripped... as she grabbed me by the mizzenmast..." A recommended read for aficionados of maritime thrillers.

The author plunges you in from the first page

I had a smile on my face through the whole reading of this exciting adventure. The author plunges you in from the first page with an exciting encounter with a Great White Shark, and does not let up until you have ridden the twists and turns to the very end. You will imagine Charley Manner right next to you, keeping you on the edge of your seat as he tells you of his adventures tangling with drug lords and alligators, with a kick-ass DEA agent and a buddy from his Navy SEALs days by his side. Charley has a delightfully dry sense of humor, and is someone I'd want on my side!

ABOUT THE AUTHOR

Michael Marnier enjoys tall tales. Reading Mark Twain's Celebrated Jumping Frog of Calaveras County at an early age made a lasting impression that set the stage for his writing style. Amp up the pace, throw in some high-tech gadgets and weaponry, substitute the frog with a man-eating shark, wrap it around an invincible hero and you have *Trouble on the Straits*. Marnier is in a comfort zone writing action adventure thrillers. He infuses his own life experiences into the main character, Charley Manner, including an encounter with something very big while SCUBA diving. The fish was not clearly visible in the murk sixty feet below the surface but imagination filled in the blanks. Marnier combined a fish-fighting chair, a bottle of tequila, a great white shark and a swash-buckling, ass-kicking former Navy SEAL for an action packed opening to his debut novel. Six feet four inches tall, 220 pounds of lean power, encased in a charbroiled tan and topped with salt-crusted hair lightened by Florida's scorching sulphur sun, Charley is larger than life. He loves to tell tall tales just like Marnier. Caution. After reading *Trouble on the Straits*, you might get hooked on the series. Check my website for updates.

http://michaelmarnier.com

Check out *Hellhole in Khyber*, the prequel to *Trouble on the Straits*.

The events in the story take place two years before *Trouble on the Straits*, Book 1 in the Charley Manner Action Adventure series, and are based on fictional special operations missions in Afghanistan prior to U.S. troop withdrawal in 2014. *Hellhole in Khyber* is a novella-length prequel in the series, which can be read and enjoyed in any order. I've made sure to exclude spoilers for those of you who haven't read Book 1 yet. Existing fans of Charley's escapades will still find plenty of fresh action and adventure, as well as a little background detail on some of the major players in the Charley Manner universe. I hope you enjoy the prequel and continue reading the series.

Prequel description: Charley Manner is separated from his SEAL team during an ambush in the Khyber Pass. His war dog is wounded and one mate is killed. The rest of the team is extracted under heavy fire, leaving Charley behind. Captured and tortured by the Taliban, he is left to die in a hole filled with human excrement and rotting body parts, deep in a cave on a Spin Ghar mountain. But Charley has other ideas.

Snag your FREE copy of the ebook by sending an email to michaelmarnier@icloud.com with HELLHOLE in the title. (Available Spring 2017)

www.ingramcontent.com/pod-product-compliance
Lightning Source LLC
Chambersburg PA
CBHW071234130626
46556CB00003B/1004

* 9 7 8 0 6 9 2 4 4 7 1 8 5 *